Red Alert

Peter Bryant

J.W. Publications

Isbn 978-0-359-21701-4

RED ALERT

☆   ☆   ☆   ☆   ☆   ☆

by

PETER BRYANT

☆   ☆   ☆

" ALABAMA ANGEL "

09.45 G.M.T.
Moscow: 12.45 p.m.
Washington: 5.45 a.m.

THE CREW of *Alabama Angel*, fourteen hours out from a Strategic Air Command base just north of Sonora, Texas, were over the hump. They were approaching the last turning point, and the boring hours which had ground round the clock face with agonising slowness in the earlier stages of the mission, now seemed to be hurrying on, allowing them to anticipate hot food and a comfortable bed, at the British base where they would spend the next two months.

It had been a long flight, and a hard one. From Sonora they had struck due north, the hours and the miles slipping away from them until, over Baffin Island, they had made their first rendezvous with a tanker. *Alabama Angel*, a B-52 type inter-continental bomber, had drunk deeply from the tanker, then hastened on to a second rendezvous over the frozen wastes between the Northeast Foreland of Greenland, and Spitzbergen.

There again a KC-135 Stratotanker had been waiting patiently for them, ready to slake the thirst of the eight great engines. Now, as the bomber approached her final turning point, she was fully topped up with fuel. There was enough in the tanks to take her on to any target assigned to her inside Russia, and still leave enough to get back to a base in the States without further refuelling.

But that was on a war mission. Today was peace, and *Alabama Angel* would merely reach her final turning point—called in Strategic Air Command jargon the X point—and turn her sleek, arrow shape away from the vitals of Russia and towards the British base where the wing of which she formed a part was being rotated on normal overseas temporary duty.

In all, thirty-two bombers of the 843rd Wing had left Sonora fourteen hours before. Like *Alabama Angel*, all of them were now a hundred miles or so from their X points. In the case of *Alabama Angel*, the X point was Bear Island, a small dot in the Barents Sea roughly midway between the northern tip of Norway and Spitzbergen. The X points of the other bombers of the wing were as widely separated as Schmidt Island in the Arctic Sea, and Bahrein in the Persian Gulf. They had only one geographical factor in common. They were all approximately two hours flying time from a Russian target of prime importance.

As the bomber approached the X point the crew began to brighten up. For hours past, conversation had been confined to the technicalities strictly necessary between crew members to keep an eight jet bomber flying. Now it became more general. The navigator was busily plotting the final course. Soon they would be on the last leg, and the boredom of the preceding hours would be forgotten in the anticipation of what was to come. Their last visit to England was still fresh in their minds.

As a matter of policy, all SAC wings were regularly rotated between their own home base in the Continental United States and bases overseas. It accustomed the crews to operating in all kinds of climate and airfield conditions. It was tough on the married men, of course, but that was the price of belonging to an élite organisation. The single men were unanimous in thinking it a great idea.

Alabama Angel's crew were all single, and they were the youngest crew on the wing, with an average age of only twenty-three. In the States they were usually kept more than busy flying simulated missions, and participating in exercises which helped to illuminate weak points in various defence organisations. Then every three or four months the wing was rotated to a SAC base overseas. It didn't leave a lot of time for the serious business of courtship and marriage. The majority of *Alabama Angel's* crew, happy with their visits to European countries, and their vivid short passes to Fort Worth, and occasionally Dallas, were not too worried about it. Captain Clint Brown, the command pilot, saw it differently. He was heavily engaged.

Brown was the daddy of the crew, at the ripe old age of twenty-six. He was a tall, heavy-set man, fair-haired, slow in speech and movement, slow to anger. The steady type. Which explained why he had been given the command of a three-million-dollar, one-hundred-and-eighty-ton bomber at an age three years less than the average age of B-52 pilots. He came from Dothan, Alabama, but he had spent most of his life before joining the Air Force in Cincinnati, which accounted for his lack of Southern accent.

Brown glanced at his watch. Before take-off he had set it to Greenwich Mean Time. When you can travel one way about as fast as the world can rotate the other, time becomes confusing. Greenwich Mean Time, besides being vital for navigational purposes, gave an established central reference point against which you could deduct or add hours to give you local time. "Time to turn, Stan?" he asked.

Lieutenant Stanley F. Andersen, twenty-three years old and *Alabama Angel's* navigator, laid his pencil down on his chart. "Thirteen minutes from now. New course will be two two zero. Estimate Lakenheath twelve thirty hours. Give or take a few minutes, natch."

Brown said: "Natch. Or a few hours maybe? How about that, men?"

"Nuts," Andersen broke in, before the chorus from the crew that sometimes greeted his estimated times of arrival could howl derisively through the intercom. "You guys tell me one time I slipped up more than five minutes." It was his invariable comeback, the one he knew they could not reasonably answer. But nevertheless they did. Earlier in the mission he would not have invited comment; earlier, the crew would not have made it. But always, just before the final turn, the holiday spirit came on them. Perhaps it was because right up to the time they reached the X point the awful fear was riding in the pressurised cabin along with them.

After X point things changed, and they were as near X point now as made no difference. Soon they would turn, and each pulse of power from the engines would be another few yards on the road to home. It made no difference whether home was North Africa, or Britain, or wherever else in the world SAC had decided to send them. Home was where they could touch down after a mission with the two unimaginable bombs that hung in the long bomb bay of the B-52 still safely in place.

To ride a few feet above an explosive power so potent that five or six B-52's could have settled World War Two decisively for either side, did not worry them. There was little risk of accidental detonation. But all of them, as part of their indoctrination, had seen the films of Hiroshima and Nagasaki. All of them had been shown the comparative strength of the puny twenty kiloton bomb dropped then, against the fifteen megaton monsters which they carried.

Sometimes they did not carry the actual bombs, but concrete replicas of the same size, shape, and weight. Then the pressure was off. The mission was a happy one. But when the wing rotated overseas, carrying of the actual weapons was mandatory, as it was on any of the training missions which took the individual aircraft to their X points. And at those times fear was an inseparable companion on the flight. Not fear for themselves but for the world.

They felt it a little less perhaps because they were single men. But still they felt it. The Air Force was perfectly aware of this. A tighter individual check was kept on SAC aircrews than on any body of men in history. And when the strain became too much, when there were signs that the human spirit could endure no more of the hideous responsibility, men were quietly relieved and re-assigned to duty where their minds could slowly come back to normal under the healing warmth of the knowledge that, for a time at least, they would not be called on to destroy upwards of five million human beings at the press of a button.

The SAC crews accepted these things as reality. They believed they guarded the peace of the world as surely as they knew the price they must pay within themselves to do it. If they had been ignorant, unintelligent men it would have been easier for them. But ignorant, unintelligent men could not have flown a jet bomber. The aircrew were highly trained men of good educational background. They could think for themselves. The Air Force preferred it that way, even if it put a limit on the number of missions and years a SAC crew might be expected to operate efficiently.

So now, as Andersen called, "Three minutes to run," and Brown set the new course on the gyro, the crew were happy. There is a peculiar intimacy which grows up between members of a bomber crew. After a few months together there is established between them an almost telepathic understanding. There was no need for anyone to ask Sergeant Garcia to break out two Thermos jugs of coffee. He knew as soon as they started on the home leg the rest of the boys, like himself, would want coffee. He reached up to the rack, and took down two jugs and a set of disposable containers. He was whistling quietly.

In the same way Garcia knew about the coffee, Lieutenant Goldsmith, the gunnery officer, knew it was time to make the introductory remarks which would set the stage for his story. Goldsmith was the established comic of the crew. He was a small, lively, intelligent-eyed man, with a devastating gift of mimicry. His stories were invariably long, involved, amatory, and very funny. He rationed them strictly to one per mission. Now he said, "Say Captain, you remember the last time we hit London?"

Brown grinned. Whatever his reply, he knew that Goldsmith's story would not concern London. It would deal with the home town or home state of one of the crew. But Goldsmith always liked to approach his story obliquely, through a series of conversational gambits as formal and as meaningless as the introductory movements of a minuet. He said, "I remember we hit London. Guess I don't remember a heck of a lot of what we did there. Why?"

The crew listened attentively. They all recognised the preliminaries. Soon they would turn, Garcia would pass the coffee round, and Goldsmith would begin the story proper. "Well," he continued, "you remember we went to that joint called the Celebrité? Just off Bond Street?"

"Sure." This was a dialogue confined to Brown and Goldsmith the crew realised, which indicated that Brown would be the target of the story. They relaxed as comfortably as they could in their seats.

"Well, you remember we met a dame there?"

"Lots of dames," Brown said affably.

"Yeah, but this particular dame. That figure, wow! That red hair, the real, deep, copper-red kind. That up from under look she kept giving me. Remember?"

"Sorry to break in," Andersen said. "Thirty seconds to run."

"Roger." Brown stretched his left hand forward ready to select the turn control on the autopilot. "Well, I think I remember her."

"Reason I asked," Goldsmith said, but this time in an accent which was pure Alabama, the kind of accent the crew were always kidding Brown he should have, "was because she put me in mind of a lil' ole gal I encountered in Dothan, Alabama. You-all know that place, Cap'n, sir?"

The crew exchanged pleased grins. With an operator like Goldsmith to entertain them for the next fifteen minutes or so, the last leg of the mission wouldn't seem long. In a few minutes they'd be having coffee. And maybe this weekend there'd be a pass to London. Life in SAC was pretty good, all right.

So now they were almost at the X point, and once again nothing had happened. They had been briefed to turn at the X, but even if their briefing had been to carry on in to the attack, they would have turned. That was the *Failsafe* procedure, the system SAC had dreamed up to prevent any accidental attack sparking off a third world war. Unless positive attack orders were received in the air, SAC aircrews were under the strictest orders to go no further than the X point. They were only too glad to obey those orders.

"Ten seconds," Andersen said. There would be nothing for him to do for a while after they turned. He settled himself comfortably to enjoy Goldsmith's story.

"Well now, Herman, seems to me I heard of it some place." Brown's voice was carefree as he poised his finger over the turn control.

Garcia began to unscrew the top of a Thermos.

Brown's finger started to move down.

There was a short clatter of morse. It lasted only ten

seconds or so. Brown delayed the movement of his finger until the message had finished.

Sergeant Mellows, the radioman, said shortly, "Message from base, Captain. Wing to hold at X points."

SONORA, TEXAS

> 09.55 G.M.T.
> *Moscow: 12.55 p.m.*
> *Washington: 4.55 a.m.*

BRIGADIER GENERAL QUINTEN, Commanding Officer of Sonora Air Force Base, looked out through the armoured glass of his office window at the brilliantly lit, empty flight lines. His 839th Wing had gone off two hours before on a series of simulated raids designed to test the efficiency of the North American Air Defence system—NORAD as it was generally called. The 843rd, on rotation overseas from Sonora, were a few minutes from their X points on the other side of the world. Only a few lame ducks and light airplanes were left.

Quinten, a tall, spare, grey-haired man, slightly stooped and with the barely discernible beginnings of a small pot belly, turned away abruptly, and walked quickly to his desk. He sank into the padded chair which he seldom left when his crews were airborne, picked up a pencil, and made a few shapeless, meaningless marks on the note pad in front of him.

The office door opened and his exec walked in, as he

was privileged to, without first knocking. Major Paul Howard, the exec, was tied to ground duty while waiting for a leg badly broken in an auto smash to heal. It was nearly well now, and Howard was counting the days until he could return to his crew. He did not enjoy staff work and administration, but he was a graduate of the National War College, a man marked for high rank in the future if he did not foul up on the way. He performed his exec's duties efficiently and well, if without any great liking for them.

He placed a sealed envelope on Quinten's desk. "My red line's still out, General," he said. "They haven't located the fault yet."

"All right, Paul." Quinten slit the envelope open neatly with an ivory paper knife, and unfolded the single sheet of paper it contained. "Let me know immediately they fix it, will you?"

"Yes, sir. Right away." Howard turned and walked out of the office, closing the door softly behind him. He was thinking how old Quinten had got to look in the two years he had known him. Too much responsibility, Howard thought, too many long hours of sweating it out at a desk while crews carried out their training missions. Quinten had children and grandchildren. At least, one grandchild. Howard smiled as he remembered the party there had been at the club to celebrate that. But his crews were his children, too. As long as they were airborne, Quinten would be awake and at work, watching the plots of their progress round the globe. And if as happened very occasionally a crew was lost through accident, Quinten suffered all the grief of a deep and personal loss.

As soon as the door shut behind Howard, Quinten read the letter from SAC. It was a personal letter from the commander. It thanked him for his work over the past four years, assigned him to duties in the Pentagon, and informed him his relief would arrive the next day. Quinten had been expecting the letter for some time. He had already heard unofficially that he was to be relieved. He knew it was right, that every day he was pushing himself a little closer to the edge of complete breakdown. But to hear about it unofficially was one thing, to see it actually in writing another. He knew the move would mean a second star on his shoulder, but the knowledge was joyless. He knew, although the Air Force did not, that he was a very sick man. The specialist he had consulted privately in Boston during his last visit there had left him in no doubt of that.

He folded the paper. It was only when he tried to replace it in the envelope that he noticed how badly his hands were shaking. Without being really conscious of it, he watched the big second hand sweep once round the dial of the electric wall clock. 09.58 G.M.T. Quinten pressed twice on the button that would summon his exec.

Howard entered the office within twenty seconds of the bell. As he came in he saw that Quinten was holding the red line telephone in his right hand. His face was very pale, Howard thought, but his voice was quite firm as he said, "I understand," and replaced on its rest the red instrument, the telephone which linked directly with SAC operations room.

Quinten took a deep breath. "Major, hold them at their X points," he said. "Use the intercom in your office, mine might be busy. Right away." His voice was calm and quiet, the impersonal voice of an officer trained to command, and experienced in the exercise of command.

Howard acknowledged the order, turned and hurried into his own office. His training forced him to pass the orders without letting his mind speculate on their implication. That could come later. For the present it was sufficient that within a minute of Quinten's order the word had gone out to the 843rd. He returned to the commander's office, and stood at the side of the desk ready for any further orders. So far he was not greatly disturbed by the order to hold. It had happened before, several times. Then it had been training, an exercise to test the efficiency of communications between base and the widely scattered bombers. Maybe this was the same.

The red line phone clamoured loudly and imperatively. Howard stiffened as Quinten reached for it. Maybe this was the call-off. But Howard thought not. He could not pin down any definite reason why he should be disturbed, yet somehow he was.

Quinten held the smooth red plastic to his ear, and listened for a few moments. His face was pale, his eyes haunted. He said, "Okay, I hear you. All right," and reached out to replace the receiver. Howard noticed his hands were shaking badly, and he had difficulty in getting the instrument back on to its cradle. And at once Howard knew that this was it. This time it was real. An attack on the United States was under way, and the bludgeon of massive retaliation was about to start its swing.

Quinten said quietly, "All right Paul, you've probably guessed. We're in a shooting war. Get the word out to the boys. Plan R. Use your office, and wait for acknowledgments. I'll bring the base to Warning Red conditions." He watched Howard swing round and walk quickly into the adjoining office.

Quinten first called the PBX. His mind was working fast, forgetting nothing. A mind not at its best, but still capable of carrying out an operational plan whose every detail was engraved on it with the heavy clarity of innumerable repetitions. He lifted the phone to the PBX, and was put through to the supervisor. He said, "This is the Commanding Officer. You recognize my voice?"

Second Lieutenant Manelli, drowsy towards the end of his spell of duty in the air conditioned PBX sunk fifty feet below administration building, forced himself to immediate alertness. "Yes, sir," he said. "I recognise your voice, General."

"All right, Manelli. I want Warning Red passed to all sections. Report back personally on any extension doesn't answer or acknowledge. Got that?"

"Sure, General. Warning Red, report back personally any extension we can't raise. Anything more, sir?" Manelli was itching to ask the C.O. if this was really it. But he didn't. Like the rest of SAC he had been trained to know that needless questions wasted precious seconds.

"Yes, there is. From here on in the base is sealed tight. That includes incoming calls, as well as outgoing. We may have to deal with saboteurs pretending to be anyone from the President down. No calls from inside go out. No calls from outside are even answered, let alone put through. *No calls*. You understand?"

"Yes, sir. No calls in or out without your personal say so."

"No calls at all, with or without my personal say so," Quinten said patiently. "My voice can be imitated too, Lieutenant."

Manelli swallowed. He was very young, and very proud of the responsible position he held on the base. He said, "No calls at all, General. Rely on me, sir."

"I will, Manelli." Quinten replaced the phone, lit a cigarette. He knew he could depend on Manelli. He was a good kid, keen on his job, not afraid of responsibility. Now, after goofing off like that, he would make sure he didn't goof again. The PBX was tight.

Quinten drew on his cigarette. He could not expect Howard back with him for three or four minutes yet. He ran briefly in his mind the main features of plan R. Then he flicked the lever of the intercom set, brought in the Communications Officer and the Tower. He said, "Close down your sections. Just as soon as all the eight forty-third have acknowledged. There'll be nothing further for you to do, so you can get below ground."

The Communications Officer, Captain Masters, said, "General, I have to ask for clarification of those orders. If I shut down, and the Tower, there'll be no radio or teleprinter communication in or out of the base. Is that your intention, sir?"

"That is. Get moving on it. And Masters."

"Sir?"

"You were quite right to ask. For your information, all that side will be handled from SAC. Now get started—Tower?"

"Sir?"

"Have all the acknowledgments come in?"

"Working on the last six, General."

"O.K. Get your personnel under ground as soon as you can."

Quinten flicked off the intercom. He thought about Masters. The Communications Officer had been absolutely correct to make sure he had understood the orders. In the same way, he felt there had been a duty on his part to convey to Masters his approval of the query. An individual infantryman saw only his small part of the battle. The commander had to take account of the whole. Masters's transmitters and receivers were his part of the battle. In the big picture, which Quinten saw over all, they had no place. Then he dismissed Masters from his mind as Howard walked back into the office. "All on their way, Paul?"

"Everyone, General. All acknowledged. General, Tower told me we're closing down on communications."

"Sure." There were a hundred and one things Quinten wanted to start on. But this was his exec. He would have to sit in on the battle. Quinten lit another cigarette. "Here's the way it is, Paul. The eight thirty-ninth will be kept airborne. No point risking them being caught on the ground. They aren't armed, but the Russians don't know that. The eight forty-third are off our hands. We won't see them back here. By the time they've hit their targets and fought their way out it should be over one way or the other. Meanwhile, we're liable to be attacked. No point in sacrificing personnel. That answer you?"

"Sure thing, sir."

"All right. Let's get to work. The base is at Warning Red. That's from SAC. In addition I want the following implemented. Double up on defence combat teams. There's no reason why there shouldn't be an attack on this base by conventional forces. All privately owned radios impounded. Air Police will have the lists of owners. Got to face the possibility of instructions to saboteurs coming over them. For the same reason, all Air Force owned radios impounded too. Those first, and fast, while I see just what we're going to hit."

Howard swung into action, flipping switches on the intercom, sometimes with a phone in each hand while he gave out orders on one, received reports on the other. Among the reports was one from PBX that the General's orders had been carried out. Every extension had been contacted and had acknowledged, the report added.

Quinten opened the safe built into the right pedestal of his steel desk. From it he took a bulky briefcase which was chained to a securing staple in the wall of the safe. He unlocked the case, fumbled inside it for a moment, then pulled out a sealed fifteen by ten envelope. He broke the seals of the envelope, and extracted a folder with a big red R stamped on it. He put the folder on his desk.

Howard replaced a phone on its rest, and made a final tick on his check list. "All cleared, General."

"Fine. I'll speak to personnel over the address system in a while. They're too busy right now." He opened the folder at the first page, scanned quickly down it. Needlessly. The words were etched indelibly on his brain. He was one of the five officers who had done the detailed planning on "R", and on several other letters too. There was no aspect of the plan with which he was not minutely familiar. He looked up at Howard. "This is the big time," he said softly. "The real big time. Moscow, Leningrad, Sverdlovsk, Stalingrad. Plus fourteen of the biggest bomber bases, the really important ones. Their one operational I.C.B.M. launching site, and the three they've almost completed. The biggest, Paul. That's why it's been assigned to the eight forty-third."

"Sure," Howard said. His own Wing was the 839th, but he recognised the rightness of Quinten's assessment. The 843rd had the B-52.K's. They were the first wing to have the K's, the only wing which was fully trained on them. It was right those targets should be assigned to the 843rd, because they were the targets that mattered. Once they were destroyed there would be no further massive attacks on the States.

At the back of his mind he was still conscious of a vague disquiet. He sought for it desperately. There was something he had to ask Quinten, he knew. His eye fell on the intelligence summary he had placed on Quinten's desk an hour earlier. He said, "Sir, that base isn't operational. The I.C.B.M. one I mean. According to today's summary, they've hit trouble. It's out for anything up to a month. Something to do with faults showing up in the metal structure of the firing pits. You read it?"

"Why no," Quinten said, "I didn't read it yet. But I can't say I'm surprised. The way they rushed the construction job through to frighten the N.A.T.O. politicians, they were bound to hit trouble some time." He got up from his desk, paced to the window, stood looking out. "That only leaves the manned aircraft: the Bison Jets and the Bear turbo-props, which means we're in with a real fighting chance. Better than evens, much better."

"Seems kind of funny though, General."

"What does?" Quinten swung round to face him.

"Well, sir, you wouldn't figure they'd pick a time their only operational missile battery that can hit the States is out. I don't get it."

"Maybe they intended us to think that way, Paul." Quinten's voice was quiet, reflective. "Maybe they thought we'd get the news and write off the threat for a week or so, lift our guard a little. It's been known to happen before in the history of war."

"Sure. I suppose so. It's peculiar, though."

Quinten smiled briefly. There was no humour in the smile, just a passing half second's bitter amusement. "They're peculiar people," he said. He was going to say something else, but again the red line phone shattered the quiet.

Howard said, "I'll get it, General," and began to walk over to the telephone.

Quinten said sharply, "Leave it to me, Major. I want to speak to the Security Officer. Personally. Have him come up, will you?" He walked back to the desk, picked off the receiver, listened to the message as Howard went out of the office. Then he began to speak.

" ALABAMA ANGEL "

10.00 G.M.T.
Moscow: 1.00 p.m.
Washington: 5.00 a.m.

THE ORDER to hold at X point left the crew of *Alabama Angel* quiet and uneasy. Like Major Paul Howard, back at Sonora, they had known it happen before. But never quite so late. Usually the warning order was issued at least twenty minutes before X point. They told themselves this was just another exercise, another of the endless variety of surprises SAC kept dreaming up to ensure that, when the time really came, nothing could surprise them. But Goldsmith did not continue with his story. Garcia slowly screwed the top of a Thermos tight again, replaced it and its companion in the rack. Nobody said anything much, because nobody wanted to risk disturbing Sergeant Mellows, the radioman. Right then, Mellows was the most important man in the crew.

Clint Brown held the plane in a steady port orbit. As soon as Mellows had passed the word to hold at X point he had taken over manual control of *Alabama Angel.* There was no particular need for him to have done it. The autopilot could hold height, speed, and rate of turn, just as well as he could. Better in fact, he thought wryly, as he noticed he had lost a hundred or so feet since he took over. He made the small correction required, and wondered just why he had taken over. He thought it was almost certainly because, if the word came, he wanted at that particular moment to have the bomber under his control as well as his command. It occurred to him he had never felt that way before when the order had come to hold, He concentrated grimly on his instruments, waiting like the rest of the crew. But with a chill presentiment that he already knew what the message would be.

Sergeant Mellows' whole being was concentrated on the green flicker of his visual tune indicator. He was very conscious that for the moment he was the centre of attention. Later his role would probably be unimportant, but for now he was carrying the ball. His sensitive, technician's fingers caressed the tune and gain controls of the receiver. For one long, frightening second he wondered whether he would suddenly forget all his training, forget his tune technique, even forget the morse code. He was the youngest of the crew, and the least experienced. He came very near to panic, until suddenly, magically, the first stammer of morse in his earphones was coming through clear and slow. He scribbled down the message letter by letter. No possibility of a mistake at that speed. He thought scornfully that the operator back at Sonora was pretty punk. He was not aware that SAC instructions limited the speed of attack orders to the equivalent of twelve words per minute. SAC did not intend to have a target spared because of an error in transmission or reception.

Mellows said, "Message from base, Captain. KNHF, AGRB." His throat was dry, and he found it difficult to speak. "That decodes as *Wing attack, plan R,* sir."

There was silence in the cabin for all of ten seconds. Goldsmith spoke first, but only because he was the first to be able to put thoughts into words. "My God no," he said, and then, as realisation grew in him that the orders could only mean an attack on the States was under way, "Where have the bastards hit? What have they. . . ."

"Shut up!" Brown's voice cut through Goldsmith's words with warning coldness. The message had not shocked Brown as much as the others, for his presentiment had warned him it was coming. Now he had to jump right in while they were still shocked, and lean on them with all the weight of his own authority and the authority behind him. He had to hit them with the single important fact that he was in command, and they obeyed him instantly, or else. That way, he would have a crew. Any other way he would have nothing but an unruly mob.

He picked on a name. Not because he expected any particular trouble from that man, in fact quite the reverse, but because it was he who had spoken first, and a specific warning to an individual is always more effective than a vague threat to a crowd. "Goldsmith," he said, "if you speak once more before I give you leave, you'll face a general court when we get back to the States." His voice was cold, and precise. It left no room for any doubt he meant exactly what he said.

He waited just long enough to make sure his warning had sunk in. Then he continued, in the same cold voice. "That goes for everyone in the crew. Let's not have it happen again."

There was silence for all of ten seconds. Goldsmith broke it. "Captain?" His voice was tentative, but quite steady now.

"Yes?"

"I was out of line. Sorry."

Brown grinned. He was grateful to Goldsmith. Quite unintentionally he had given Brown the chance to weld the crew into a tight combat team right at the start, to get them over the inevitable initial shock of the attack orders. Brown thought he could ease off now with perfect safety provided he got them busy right away on their combat duties.

He said, "That's O.K., Herman. Forget it. Break out the orders, Stan. Garcia, you distribute them."

Stan Andersen unlocked the metal drawer built in under his chart table. It contained half a dozen fifteen by ten envelopes exactly the same in appearance as the one Quinten had opened. Altogether SAC had twenty-one alternative plans, lettered from A through U. But of those, only six applied to the 843rd. Their targets were the vital ones, simply because they had the most modern, best defended bombers in the Command. If any bombers flying could fight their way through the supersonic fighters, the ground and air launched missiles, which the Russians had sited to defend those targets, the 52.K's could. So naturally, the vital targets were theirs.

Andersen broke the seals on the envelope marked "R". The others he had already replaced in the steel drawer. It contained an incendiary device which could be operated manually in event of emergency, and would be set off by an inertia switch in event of the bomber crashing.

Garcia distributed the individual folders. There was one each for radar and radio; one for the gunnery officer, the engineer, the bombardier. One for each of the two crew members whose duties would begin and end with twenty minutes' work a few hundred miles from the target. And for the navigator and the captain, a copy each of a bulkier folder which included the orders for the other crew members as well as their own.

Brown glanced quickly at his orders, saw that he did not need to alter height or speed on the first leg, and said, "First course as soon as you like, Stan. Don't wait to plot it, a rough heading will do."

"Kay. Roughly zero seven five."

"Zero seven five." Brown glanced at his heading indicator. Two three zero. He increased the rate of port turn, the servo controls calling for no more effort from him to tilt the huge swept back wings than he could supply with the tip of a finger. He rounded out of the turn, made the inevitable small correction, and said, "Steady on zero seven five."

Andersen noted the time, set his ground position indicator to the co-ordinates of Bear Island, and fed into the machine the wind velocity he had computed on the run up to the X point. The speed and height were already set. From now on the gadget would automatically compute his ground position, and display it in everchanging co-ordinate figures. Provided of course, that the wind and speed Andersen fed in was accurate. A large provision at fifty-five thousand feet. His busy fingers moved rapidly over the chart, measured distances and angles, transmuted them into marks on a spherical slide rule, noted the resultant figures on his log. He had quite forgotten his girl in Klamath Falls, Oregon. It was not a likely target.

Brown's girl lived in Seattle. He had met her when, with other 843rd pilots, he had gone to the Boeing plant for a three day conference on certain tricky points which had shown up after the 52.K's had flown five or six training missions. She worked as a stenographer in the accounts offices there. A tall, lissom brunette, the girl he had planned to marry at the end of his next overseas duty. He tried to put out of his mind the knowledge that Seattle and the Boeing plant would certainly be a priority target. He succeeded, but only by plunging into the detailed check of crew assignments.

First communications. "Mellows, you got the acknowledgment off?"

"Yes, sir. Aircraft number and the second group. AGRB. Like we were briefed."

"O.K. Check these points. Complete radio silence. Listen on what wavelength?"

"Nine two one five kay-cees, Captain. That's a frequency, not a wavelength."

Brown smiled. "Too technical for me. All right, code procedure?"

"I'll read out what it says. To ensure the enemy cannot plant false transmissions and fake orders, once the attack orders have been passed and acknowledged the CRM 114 is to be switched into the receiver circut. The three code letters of the period are to be set on the alphabet dials of the CRM 114, which will then block any transmissions other than those preceded by the set letters from being fed into the receiver. I've set up the CRM, Captain."

"O.K., Mellows. Engineer?"

Master Sergeant Federov, three generations removed from the vast grain lands of the Ukraine, a taciturn, sturdy man whose only love was the smooth efficiency of *Alabama Angel's* infinitely complex machinery, grunted his presence.

"No change yet. Check with me five minutes before point A. Bombardier?"

Lieutenant Harry Engelbach, not as taciturn as Federov, quiet in normal social intercourse because of an overwhelming shyness, had lost all trace of that reticence now. He said, "Primary target the I.C.B.M. base at Kotlass, Captain. One weapon, fused air burst at twenty thousand. Second weapon to be used if there's any foul up with the first. Otherwise, the secondary target gets it. The supply centre for the Kotlass base just outside Archangel. Fused air burst at twenty five."

"O.K. You have your target approach maps?"

"Yes. Approach and vicinity charts and transparencies for both. Kotlass should be easy, Captain. The aiming point is almost at the junction of the Dwina and Suchona rivers. They'll show up real clear on the scope."

"Let's hope so. Gunnery?"

"Gunnery," Goldsmith said. His voice was calm and steady, differing from normal in the absence of the flippant bantering note that usually was present.

"O.K. Herman, nothing for you yet. You can arm your hornets up ten minutes before A point. You happy about them?"

"I'm happy. I'd be happier if we could carry twice as many, but these ten beauties should do. I'll check with you before I arm them."

"O.K. Herman. Radar, you stay on search for now. You don't begin counter measures until we turn in on the attack leg. We'll check the counter-frequencies when I've altered course. How about it, Stan? You have that course for me?"

Andersen noted a final figure on his log, and said, "Zero eight one. Alter fifty seconds from now."

"Roger." Brown leaned forward to make the alterations on the gyro. There were only two of the crew he had to contact now; Garcia, and another sergeant named Minter. They had flown a lot with *Alabama Angel*, but neither of them had yet contributed anything more positive to the actual operation of the plane than serve coffee. Yet, without them, the present mission could not have been ordered.

"Ordnance?"

"Sir?" It was Garcia who answered, as he always did. Garcia was the live wire of the pair, a girl chaser, a likeable, volatile man. But from past experience Brown knew that Minter would be listening, and would carefully carry out any orders he was given.

"As soon as the navigator comes up with an estimate for A point, I'll let you know about your job."

"Estimating 10.41 at A point," Anderson broke in quickly.

"Give or take anything?" Brown asked lightly. There was an appreciative chuckle from the crew. Brown was pleased. This was the delicate part, the instructions which might trigger again the emotional disturbance which had threatened when the attack orders were received. He went on quickly, "Don't answer that, Stan. Only kidding. All right, you two, you can begin to arm them up at 10.33. Number one for twenty thousand air burst, number two twenty-five air burst." Now. It was said. Any comment from the crew? Five seconds went by. None. Brown smiled again. He thought a cup of coffee would be good right now. "How about some coffee, Garcia?"

"Right away, Captain."

Minter said slowly, "Hey Garcia, Bim for twenty air and Bam for twenty-five air, that right?"

"Sure," Garcia said, "that's right."

Brown was staggered. He could understand how the crews of previous wars had often chalked names on high explosive bombs. But to give names to these things? He started to ask a question, changed his mind before the words had left his mouth. The bombs were Garcia's and Minter's special charges. The two sergeants had to arm them, convert them from inert if highly expensive chunks of metal, into killers with a power potential capable of removing a city the size of New York from the face of the earth. If they liked to give the weapons names that was none of his business, so long as their job was efficiently done. He felt quite sure it would be.

Two minutes later, while the crew read carefully through their assignment sheets, Garcia served the coffee. But Goldsmith did not tell his story, and nobody invited him to tell it. There seemed to be a tacit agreement the story would not be at all funny. Not now.

SAC Hq. OMAHA, NEBRASKA

10.05 G.M.T.
Moscow: 1.05 p. m.
Washington: 5.05 a.m.

AT A HUNDRED listening posts throughout the free world, in hot climates and in cold, out of scorching desert and arctic tundra, the slender radio masts lift their receiving aerials high into the air. These are the stations which maintain a guardian watch, picking up signals from airborne bombers, and sometimes signals from the ground to those bombers. They are the junction points of the invisible spider's web of radio. They cover the whole of the northern hemisphere and ninety per cent of the southern. They never sleep.

Seven of them received the attack orders to the 843rd Wing. A further four heard the acknowledgment signals from the bombers. Within minutes the signals had been filtered through the listening stations' sector centres, back through the main area centres, to arrive with a clatter of teletype machines at SAC's command post in Omaha, Nebraska.

Here again the signals were filtered. They passed through the decoding room, where individual airmen automatically channelled them to the duty officer, as standing orders required when signals included any form of attack instructions. He in turn routed them on to the duty operations officer. Exactly six minutes after the attack orders had gone out from Sonora the first plain language transcript landed on the duty operations officer's desk. Three minutes later, the last of the individual acknowledgments had landed there too.

The duty operations officer never ranked below full colonel. He had immense discretionary powers. In certain circumstances he could order SAC into the air before obtaining authority from the commander or his deputy. Naturally, he would be called upon to justify such an action when he notified the commander. But if he could prove the emergency was such he felt it right to issue the orders without wasting the two or three minutes which might be necessary to locate the commander and obtain his approval, then his action would be affirmed.

The duty colonel read the first transcript, then dropped it to look intently at the threat board, which was kept up to date at two-minute intervals on information supplied over a closed circuit from NORAD. He read two or three of the acknowledgment transcripts, while he considered his course of action. The SAC commander was in Washington, but the deputy was sleeping peacefully a few hundred feet above the colonel's head.

The colonel instructed his assistant, a grey haired major without wings who looked after administration and staff details, to get the deputy commander down without delay. Then he picked up the red line phone and asked the operator to get him Sonora. He was a few years junior to Quinten, but ten years previously he had served with him in Berlin. He knew Quinten well, and liked and respected him. In under ten seconds he heard Quinten on the line. He said, "General, duty operations SAC. We have some transcripts of signals supposed to have been exchanged between Sonora and the eight forty-third wing. Did you know about them?"

He listened intently as Quinten began to speak. For half a minute he listened, then held the phone away from his ear after the click from the other end told him Quinten had cut off. He flashed the operator, said urgently: "Get the deputy at Sonora on the second line."

The operator said, "Pardon me, Colonel, there's no deputy

at Sonora right now, he's gone to England with the eight forty-third. The exec's sitting in as deputy for a few days. Major Howard."

"Howard? Oh sure." The colonel knew Howard about as well as he knew Quinten. "Get me Howard, then."

"No can do, Colonel. That line's out. There's been a fault on it the last two hours. Matter of fact, General Quinten was worried about it. Got me to check his own line."

"O.K." He replaced the phone and sat thinking for a long minute. Then he glanced at the threat board again. Nothing seemed to have changed. He began to give orders. All SAC bases to immediate readiness. Crews to be briefed, and planes positioned at the end of runways with full war load. Establish contact with Sonora through the normal PBX, personal call to Major Howard. Stratotanker bases alerted for maximum effort, every KC-135 they had to be ready to go. Establish contact with Sonora by radio and teletype. All SAC wings already airborne with war load to head for nearest tanker rendezvous. The SAC commander in Washington to be located wherever he might be. There were dozens of details to be seen to, he didn't know quite how many. He was ploughing steadily through them when the deputy commander arrived..

Very quickly, he outlined what was going on, what he had done. While he was talking he was interrupted twice. Once to say it was impossible to raise Sonora by radio or teletype. No response to signals. Again to inform him Sonora PBX was not accepting inward calls.

The deputy commander was a two star general. He could go way further than a colonel. And did. Two more wings were ordered off, with instructions to head north. Later orders would reach them by the time they got to one of the tanker rendezvous areas. All overseas SAC bases were brought to immediate readiness. Ent Air Force Base at Colorado

Springs was contacted, and the NORAD headquarters there alerted to the possibility of enemy air attack. NORAD took the alert in its stride. A major air exercise was already in progress. SAC called off the attacking forces. NORAD brought in all its fighters for refuelling and arming, and ordered the Distant Early warning stations from Cape Lisburne to Baffin Island to warning red.

General Franklin, the SAC commander, was located in Washington. The general had attended a long and boring dinner the previous evening. He had a slight hangover and he was not in the best of moods. He demanded to know why the hell he'd been dragged out of bed at that hour.

The deputy commander told him. The two generals spoke for perhaps forty seconds, and then the deputy commander turned to the duty operations officer. "General Franklin wants to hear from you just what Quinten said. Try to remember his exact words."

The colonel took the phone. "Sir, I asked General Quinten if he knew about the orders received and acknowledged by the eight forty-third wing. As near as I can get to his words, he replied, '*Sure, the orders came from me. They're on their way in, and I advise you to get the rest of SAC in after them. My boys will give you the best kind of start. And you sure as hell won't stop them now.*'"

SONORA, TEXAS

10.15 G.M.T.
Moscow: 1.15 p.m.
Washington: 5.15 a.m.

". . . how the enemy will come or when. Maybe as a missile from a submarine lying off coast. Because of our geographical position I doubt that, but we can't ignore the possibility. Maybe it will be a four-jet Bison or a turbo-prop Bear, with the same kind of weapons we carry in our fifty-two. Well, the NORAD boys are no slouches. I hate to say it as a SAC man, but I wouldn't be too happy if we were assigned the task of breaking through the NORAD defence lines in time of war. They're that good.

"Some of you men listening to me are probably saying about now—sure, that's great, so we stop the bombers. How do we stop the inter-continental ballistic missiles? Well, I want to assure you all, and especially those of you who have homes maybe, or friends, in the big cities. You don't have to worry about the I.C.B.M. It won't be hitting us. I can't reveal just how we know it, but you have my promise we do.

"There is another form of attack, though, which I think might be the most dangerous one for us here. I mean a conventional attack, whether by individual saboteurs or large armed parties. That's the reason I've doubled up on the defence combat teams. Men, I want to impress on you the need for watchfulness. The enemy will try any tricks to fool you into letting him on the base. He may come individually, or he may come in strength. He may well come in the uniform of our own combat troops. But however he comes, we have to stop him.

"I'm going to give you three simple rules. The first is to truth no-one, whatever his uniform, whatever his rank, who is not known to you personally. The second is anyone or anything that approaches within two hundred yards of the perimeter is fired on. And the third—if in doubt, fire anyway. I would sooner accept a few casualties through accident than lose a whole base and its personnel through over-caution.

"That's about all I have to say except for two small points. Any variation on the rules I have given you must come from me. Personally. I want that clearly understood. There are no exceptions to it, whatever the circumstances. And last of all, I know you are all worried about your families both on the base here and all over our country. Well, let's make sure we defend the families here on the base. Because you can depend on it that other Americans are defending your families elsewhere with the same unyielding spirit we're going to show here at Sonora. Good luck to you all."

Quinten flicked off the tab of the address system. He had stood up to speak, and now he sank wearily into the chair behind his desk. He lit a cigarette. Well, he thought, it was done now. The attack was launched. The base was tightly sealed. He felt that he could pillow his head on his hands and sleep right there at his desk for a week. But his tautly strung nerves would not let him relax. His weary brain, against his conscious will, began once more to review the plan and its implementation, seeking for any flaw in its conception or execution.

The plan was founded on two well-established concepts. The first was that a military force which is poised for attack, can often be knocked off balance by an opponent who himself attacks without warning.

The Russians' main strength lay in the fact they could select at their leisure the time and place of the attack. They could launch the attack with their defences fully prepared for the American counter-punch. Quinten reasoned that if the Americans, instead of counter-punching after a Russian attack, launched their own attack first, the Russian guard would be down. The American attack would catch them off balance, because their war plan called for instant readiness of defences only after they themselves had struck the first, devastating blow.

The Russian war plan, indeed, visualised no great threat to their own defences, for its essence was the destruction at a first blow, of almost the entire offensive power of the free world. To achieve this, the plan divided the targets to be hit into two distinct classes.

The first of these classes comprised all targets within fifteen hundred miles of Russia, or the satellite countries. That meant within intermediate missile and supersonic fighter-bomber range. The Russians had plenty of both types of weapon. The targets included all SAC bases in the Mediterranean, the Sixth Fleet, and the air forces of all European and Middle East NATO countries. The Russian missile and fighter-bomber strength was so great that their planners had decided a complete kill of such targets was as certain as anything in war ever can be. With the strictly military targets would go such cities as London, Paris, and Rome. The destruction of the cities was not regarded as essential, except in one case. They would be destroyed to assist in the general disruption of communications. The exception was London. The Russians were under no illusion about the fighting qualities of the British. A considerable proportion of their missile and fighter-bomber strength would be devoted to London, and to the offensive bases of all kinds in Britain.

For a long time it had been within the capability of Russia to destroy the first class of targets, all of them short to medium range. But their destruction was meaningless without the simultaneous destruction of the second class of targets.

These were primarily the SAC bases in the Continental United States, the SAC bases on distant islands like Okinawa, and Washington, New York, and Chicago. The weapons selected by the Russians for these targets included a fleet of submarines equipped to launch rocket missiles while still submerged, two specially trained air regiments of Bison four-jet bombers, and a minimum of thirty-six I.C.B.M.'s. At the time Quinten launched the 843rd against its targets, the Russians were only a matter of weeks from having the required total of I.C.B.M.'s operational and aimed. The American inter-continental missile, though coming along fast, was not yet operational.

The plan was simple enough. The submarines would lie in wait off Florida and in the Gulf of Mexico. They would have to be at least two hundred miles off short to escape detection, and this would cut their accuracy down. But when each of the sixty submarines allocated to the task had fired off the three missiles it carried, the destruction of two thirds of SAC bases in Continental America was a certainty. Only those bases more than two hundred miles from the coast would survive.

The two Bison regiments of fast four-jet bombers would fly a strictly one-way mission. They would strike deep into the South Pacific to evade the NORAD Mid-ocean and Offshore lines, and by accepting the mission as one way, and the regiments as expended from the time they took off, obtain the range necessary to hook at the soft underbelly of the North American continent. They would come in across Mexico under cover of darkness, drop to low altitude, and attack at full power with after-burners blasting, completely regardless of fuel consumption. The Russian staff considered that only three or four SAC bases which had escaped the missiles from the submarines, would remain unharmed.

But three or four bases were too much. Those bases could launch a retaliatory blow big enough to obliterate Russia. As far as America was concerned, they represented the ultimate deterrent. So for the ultimate deterrent, the ultimate weapon would be used. The Russian I.C.B.M.—it had been designated the M-241—was accurate only to within ten miles at long range. So to each of the four surviving bases, the Russian staff had allocated five of the monstrous rockets. Four would go to Okinawa, together with a splinter group of twelve Bisons from the main force. One each to Washington, New York, and Chicago. And finally, one each to the nine SAC bases which were just outside the certain hit range of the submarines.

The attacks would be timed to allow the Bisons to operate in darkness. That alone would increase their chances of reaching their targets by thirty per cent. They would also be timed to ensure that the counter-punch from any SAC wings already airborne at the time of the attack would have to be made in daylight. The aggressor chooses the time of the attack. It is his prerogative. Obviously he chooses a time that will help him and hinder the enemy.

Throughout the whole plan the timing would be such that the missiles would hit their targets at the same moment the attacking aircraft first appeared on the defensive radar screens. The plan was ready, the staff work and logistic preparations complete.

Except for one weapon.

The Russian I.C.B.M., after a spectacular start, had hit snags. They were being overcome, but for a short while yet their I.C.B.M. strength would be under what the Marshals considered necessary for absolute certainty. Anything less than certainty was unacceptable.

The only counter-punch left after the attack would be any SAC wings which happened to be both airborne and armed. The probability was that not more than one wing would fulfil both those conditions. They would strike back, but with everything stacked against them. They would have no darkness to cover them. They would have to fight every inch of the way to the vital targets through defences already alerted and concentrated round those targets. The Russians would concede them the non-vital ones. And finally, even if they fought through and delivered their weapons, they would have no bases to return to. They would have administered a certain amount of punishment. The Russians thought they were able to absorb that amount, especially since they knew it was the last they would be called upon to take.

Quinten had long ago reached the conclusion that the Russian plan was entirely feasible. He considered there was only way to defeat it, and that was to beat the Russians to the punch, and catch them with their guard down. It was his belief that the 843rd Wing on its own could destroy the Russian capacity to wage a global war. It was not a wild belief, but the carefully considered conclusion of a man with a lifetime's experience of bomber operations.

Everything was on the American side. The Russian defences would not be at immediate readiness. There was no reason for it. Their part in a global war had already been defined for them by the rulers of Russia as immediate readiness to deal with the counter-blow that would follow the Russian attack. They were no doubt highly competent in that role. But the whole theory of Russian military preparedness was predicated on the assumption that the West would not launch a thermo-nuclear war until after massive aggression by themselves. It gave them great advantages as long as the assumption was true. At that moment it no longer was. At one stroke their advantages had disappeared, and their defences would have only the time their radar could give them to prepare to meet the attack. Quinten was confident that time would not be sufficient.

The second concept on which Quinten had based his plan was one which is at the very heart of military theory. The soldier obeys his commander. He obeys the commander unquestioningly, not through fear of punishment, but because he has confidence and trust in his commander's judgment based on experience of, and respect for, the commander's actions in the past.

It need not be a long past. Great leaders have been known to win the confidence and devotion of their men within a few hours of taking command. Coversely, a bad commander can as quickly wreck the morale and discipline of good fighting outfits. Quinten was not a bad commander: he was in fact an extremely good one. The men under him liked him personally, respected his judgment, and obeyed him implicitly. There was never any question but they would immediately carry out the orders which had not only launched the 843rd against their targets, but also sealed off Sonora completely from the outside world.

Fate had played its part in Quinten's decision, too. On this particular morning everything was perfectly attuned to the sucessful execution of a plan he had long cherished.

Thus, the 843rd were not only airborne, but carrying the weapons. Quinten's deputy, who might have been suspicious of some of his actions, was along with the wing. The time at which the bombers would reach their X points meant they could attack in the gathering gloom of a winter evening, while surviving Russian bombers would have to hit back in daylight if they were to hit back at all. The report on the one fully operational Russian I.C.B.M. site had removed his last doubt, which was whether his bombers could smear it before the missiles were fired off. And, most important of all, the letter from SAC had shown him that this was his last chance to put the plan into action.

The soldier obeys his commander. Yes, so long as he has faith in that commander. Even after he has lost faith, discipline and training will exact his obedience for a while. Superficially, he will remain as good a soldier as before. But only superficially. When the pressure is put on him he will crumple. And when he crumples he is liable to do anything.

Quinten's position vis-à-vis the Pentagon and the statesmen who ruled America, was much the same as the ordinary airman's at Sonora to himself. But Quinten had long lost faith in the higher echelons. He did not blame the generals above him so much as the statesmen above them. He knew that some of the generals were entirely of his way of thinking, that they would have considered his plan logical, inexpensive, and entirely necessary. He blamed them only because they let the statesmen force handicap after handicap upon them.

But they were in no position to act for themselves. Quinten was. He was the commander of one of the biggest bases in the Air Force. Once that base was sealed off, he was as great a power as the captain of a ship, with as great a freedom of action, and the whole weight of established authority vested in his judgment.

The situation was not unique. Captains of naval vessels had acted in the past as Quinten was acting now. So had military commanders in the field. Their actions had usually been costly, but the cost was capable of measurement in ordinary terms. They entailed the lives of a few thousand men, the destruction of a small town, the unnecessary sinking of a nine-thousand-ton cruiser. Disastrous actions, but actions which entailed losses in terms which could be comprehended.

Quinten, on the other hand, had committed himself to action at a fateful moment in history. If his bombers all hit their targets, they could not reasonably be expected to kill less than thirty to forty million people. In theory, his action was no different from any of the similar actions which had preceded it. In practice, the past actions of commanders acting independently paled to insignificance beside it.

He allowed his head to sink on to his hands for a moment. The pain which had been an ever present companion over the past two years was worse than ever today. He thought that maybe to talk to Howard a while would help. He raised his head slowly, painfully, and reached out to the button. He remembered the red line phone, and clicked the switch attached to the scrambler box into the off position. Then he pressed the button.

Howard, sitting at his desk alert for any summons from the General, rose abruptly to his feet when he heard the signal. The niggling question that had been in his mind thrust itself forward again, demanding his attention. He started for the door, turned abruptly as realisation struck him, and walked back to his desk. He slid open the second drawer of the right hand pedestal, revealing a portable radio. It was the battery operated, transistor kind. He switched it on, listened to the local disc jockey for a few moments, then tuned in other stations. A frown spread slowly over his face. The bell rang again. He slammed the drawer shut. Then he walked slowly across the room and pushed open the door into the general's office. There were some questions he had to have answered. Urgently.

THE PENTAGON, WASHINGTON D.C.

10.25 G.M.T.
Moscow: 1.25 a.m.
Washington 5.25 a.m.

IT HAS OFTEN BEEN SAID that the Pentagon is not so much a building as a city. Certainly in terms of size and working population it merits that description. Like most other cities it is busier by day than by night. Except in time of crisis, few lights burn through the night. But ten minutes after General Franklin had received the message from Omaha, lights were winking on all over the vast building as key personnel, abruptly woken, began to arrive at their desks.

The organisation was sufficiently smooth, the communicattions system sufficiently sensitive, for the key men to be located at once. When located, they were merely given the one word which indicated a national emergency. They scrambled into their clothes, ignoring such formalities as washing and shaving. There were razors and washing facilities at the Pentagon they could use later. For now, all that mattered was to arrive at their desks fast. At that time of morning traffic was light. Even those living twenty miles out, by driving at eighty and ninety on the almost deserted highways, were able to report within fifteen minutes of the summons. Many got to their posts inside ten minutes, a few inside five. Some, of course, were already sleeping in the building.

The Joint Chiefs arrived at the War Room, half way down the central corridor, almost simultaneously. Their I.D. cards, special passes, and War Room entry permits, were scrutinised as minutely and thoroughly by the Military Police on duty outside the door as those of the more junior officers of all three services who followed them in. Nor were the elaborate security measures unnecessary. Secrets were made in other places. Here in the War Room, they were displayed.

At one end of the huge, rectangular room, a dozen comfortable arm chairs were arranged in a semi-circle facing a wall which sloped at an incline of about fifteen degrees towards the chairs. On it were three maps, all of them of the world, but drawn in such a way that the average person would not have realised at a first glance exactly what they were.

The map on the left was the least confusing. It showed density of populations, amount of food production per head of those populations, political allegiance, and degree of industrialisation. The map on the right was concerned with naval and military dispositions. At a glance it was possible to see the trend of Russian naval traffic, and the deployment of their massive land forces.

The central map, larger than both the others together, was a view of the northern hemisphere as it might have been seen from a satellite a thousand miles above the North Pole. Here were marked in red and blue the targets in Russia and America which had been allotted a priority of one or two.

Red was for priority one targets. It indicated a target which was considered vital to either side for immediate operations, and especially for offensive operations. Priority one targets were those which *must* be hit within hours of the start of a war. They consisted largely of airfields, missile sites, and a few great cities. There were forty-six such targets in America, and a further fourteen—mostly SAC bases—in the rest of the free world. In Russia there were thirty-one, with three in the satellite countries and one in China.

Priority two targets were shown in blue. They were the targets which would be hit in the second phase, between twelve hours and four days after the initial attacks. They comprised communications systems, industrial complexes, cities with a population of a half million or more, defensive airfields and missile sites. There were around five hundred of them in the free world, four hundred in the Russian bloc.

The difference between red and blue, between priority one and priority two targets, had been defined by an Air Force general back in 1951. *"These targets are all vital targets. They are all necessary in order to wage war. But first priority must surely be given to those targets which enable a nation to wage immediate offensive war. Those are priority one. In the long run the other targets may enable a nation to hurt its enemy equally badly if they are spared. But not immediately, in the first few hours. They will not be spared of course, but though they must be destroyed the need to destroy them has not the same urgency as is the case with targets in the first priority. To those targets the maximum initial effort of the attacking forces must be applied. The true test is to assume that all such targets were blotted out in a sudden attack. Could the attacked nation then mount any sort of immediate counter attack? If the answer is yes, that nation contains targets which have not been given a high enough priority. Again, assume that from among the priority one targets, each single target in turn alone comes through a sudden attack undamaged. Could an immediate counter attack be launched from that target? If the answer is no, then that target has been overgraded and belongs among the priority twos, not the priority ones."*

Behind the wall, which was made of a transparent material, teams of plotters were at work, drawing in with coloured wax pencils the X points and target routes of the 843rd Wing. Every one of the targets was shown in red. And between the thirty-two bombers, every red target was covered,

either as a primary or secondary. Quinten had been well a-
ware of that when he made his decision.

The Joint Chiefs of Staff conferred for a few moments,
talking in low tones. Then General Franklin was asked to
explain what had happened, and give his estimate of the
situation over the next two hours.

Franklin stepped up on the platform which ran the width
of the wall, and stood under the central map. He was a short,
thickly built man, with a round, impassive face. He was un-
shaven, but his plentiful black hair was neatly brushed. He
gave an impression of solid strength, and that impression
was fully in accordance with his character. Without it, he
could never have become SAC's commander in his fortieth
year.

He said, "Gentlemen, thirty minutes ago, without any orders or authorisation, one of my base commanders sent out
attack orders to a wing under his command. The wing concerned was on a simulated mission which took them to the
point where, in time of war, they could have begun the first
part of their attack procedure. In Strategic Air Command
we call this point the X point.

"You will see plotted on the map above me the thirty-
two X points of the 843rd Wing. From those points the black
lines indicate the route of each individual bomber to its
target. You will see that every red, that is priority one target,
is included in those assigned to the wing. As of this moment,
ten thirty-one Greenwich Mean Time, every bomber is between ninety and one hundred minutes flying time from
its target.

"There is a particular reason why all the priority one targets have been assigned to the 843rd. It is the one SAC wing
which is equipped with the new B-52K types. That means
it is the one wing we feel very confident is able to fight its
way through and take out all the assigned targets without

exception. Until the supersonic B-58 comes into operational use later this year, the 52.Ks are the best we've got. They are crammed with electronic devices capable of throwing off track all known Soviet guided missiles, and they carry their own air to air missiles for defense against fighters. Some of you here will already know that tests against live targets over the Gulf lead us to expect a ninety-eight per cent kill rate against attacking fighters.

"As regards offensive strength, each bomber is carrying two weapons of fifteen megaton yield. This power ensures all targets will be taken out if the bombing error does not exceed three miles, and the majority if it does not exceed five. We do not believe it will in fact exceed one mile.

"To sum up, I consider the 843rd will reach and hit its targets. All of them. That means in something under two hours from now Soviet offensive capability will be effectively destroyed. I'll answer any questions I can."

There was a low buzz of conversation in the room, mostly from the small groups of aides and staff officers. Franklin stood impassive on the platform. His face was quite expressionless. No-one could possibly have known the thoughts that were chasing through his mind. He felt deep down that, maybe Quinten was right, that this could be the only possible solution for the free world. But he gave no outward indication of his feeling.

Navy got in the first question. Admiral Maclellan was not the typical sea dog one visualised as Chief of Naval Operations. He was slight, almost delicate in build, with a sharp featured, intelligent face. "I take it there's some technical reason you can't just recall the wing?" he asked.

Franklin said bluntly, "There is. The base commander concerned picked one of the emergency plans which envisaged a commander having to act on his own because the higher echelons had been knocked out by sudden attack. He selected a plan which requires recall orders, or any orders at all, to be preceded by a three-letter group, once the initial attack instructions have been given. Without that group, the planes cannot receive the message. To guard against possible sabotage, the letters are given to the crews by the commander personally at the briefing. He and his deputy keep the letters involved a secret between them. In this case the deputy is along with the wing. And the commander refuses to recall the planes. Does that answer you, Admiral?"

"Certainly," Maclellan said. "Who is the base commander, by the way?"

Franklin hesitated. He looked towards the Air Force Chief of Staff, General Steele. Steele nodded. Franklin said slowly, "It was the base commander of Sonora, Brigadier General Quinten."

There was a low murmur round the room. Several of the Air Force officers present knew Quinten, and one or two of them knew him well. Their remarks were cut short as the Army Chief of Staff, General Keppler, growled, "You mean your system's loose enough to let a thing like this happen? No safeguards against it?" His tone implied this was just the kind of thing he expected from Air Force. He was a big, burly man, a brilliant commander of armour who had come up the hard way by serving an apprenticeship as one of Patton's column commanders, and then made a name when the Korean fighting was at its most bitter. He admired the Air Force for its close support of infantry and armour in the field, and detested the whole conception of SAC. Now he glowered steadily at Franklin.

The SAC general fought down the quick surge of anger he felt rising inside him. He considered Keppler a bigot and an archaic relic, who had failed utterly to grasp the new global strategy. But this was not the time for futile bickering and argument. He said quietly, "General, no system yet devised is proof against any and all human failings. SAC plans were as accident proof as they could reasonably be made."

"*Reasonably accident proof*," Keppler said loudly. "That isn't what you put out in the press releases back in the spring of '58. When that storm blew up over your planes hauling the actual weapons over the Pole and heading towards Russia. There was supposed to be a marvellous system to prevent this sort of thing. Failsafe or something like that. What's happened to it? Did it ever exist? Or was it just something Air Force dreamed up for the benefit of the newspapers and Congress?"

"It exists." Franklin's voice was still quiet. He was not going to let Keppler goad him into losing his temper. "What we released to the press was entirely true. But it wasn't the entire truth. It couldn't be."

"Why not?"

"Funnily enough, because we are dedicated to the principle of retaliation rather than original aggression. We accept that we will receive the first blow. Naturally, we hope our defences will be tight enough so that blow doesn't knock us right out of the ring. But to be completely realistic our plans had to take into account the possibility that first blow might be really devastating. You'll concede there is that possibility, General?"

"I will," Keppler said shortly.

"All right then, let's look at the position might arise. Washington and Omaha gone. Communications hopelessly snarled up. No central direction left. Yet the probability is that somewhere in the U.S.A. one or possibly more of our offensive bases would survive. A base commander might well find himself the only surviving officer with an effective force. There might be no command left to which he could look for orders. His communications might be completely disrupted, and his base entirely cut off from the rest of the world.

"Obviously, in a position like that, he would have to be empowered to act on his own initiative. Plan R provided for just that situation. Now the commander at Sonora has used it. We don't know why, we only know the human element has failed us. The risk was always there but it had to be accepted, because only by its acceptance could we guarantee an aggressor would never escape retaliation *so long as one of our bases, or even one of our wings, survived.* We accepted a risk, and we lost out. That's all."

Keppler grunted. In spite of his feelings about SAC he was a fair man. He appreciated a situation might arise where it would be necessary to plan for a base commander being able to act independently. That way, an error away from the enemy could be prevented. But in every case like that there was an inevitable risk of an error towards the enemy. It was slight, it was infinitesimal even, but it was there. Obviously in this case a combination of circumstances had given the commander a chance to make that error. Later, he would make sure the reason that particular commander had been left in command was fully examined. The Air Force weren't going to bury that one. But for the present, it didn't matter. The error had been made, the action taken, a SAC wing committed to battle. In his opinion here was little to be decided. The action they should take now was quite clear cut.

His train of thought was interrupted by Steele's quiet voice. Steele, in his capacity of chairman of the joint chiefs for that period, put into words the conclusions which Navy and Army were reaching independently. "Gentlemen, the President and the Secretaries of State and Defence will be joining us in a few minutes. I can see only two alternatives to suggest to them. The first is we recall the 843rd. I don't know how we can, but that is one possibility. The other," he paused, and for a few moments the room was very still. "The other," he repeated, "is to carry this action to its logical end. General Franklin has told us it is his belief the bombers already committed to attack can effectively destroy the Russian priority one targets. What guarantee can you give us of that, Franklin?"

Franklin looked up at Steele. "No guarantee, sir," he said. "I can only say I myself am confident my crews will get there and bomb accurately. It's early morning here, gentlemen, but in Russia it's getting on for dark, especially in the more northerly parts where most of the targets lie. That's an advantage we hadn't planned on. Again, there's no reason to suppose their defences are at top line. And this particular wing is considered able to hit their targets in daylight with the defences fully alert. I won't give a guarantee because I feel in war nothing can be guaranteed. Let's just say I feel confident they'll make it. One hundred per cent."

"Seems to answer that one," Maclellan said. "So what's the next step? We can't recall, apparently. All right, if we're committed let's hit them good. What else have we got?"

Keppler said, "I agree. But isn't there any chance at all of recalling them?"

Steele shook his head slowly. "We already have operators working steadily through the three-letter combinations. Trouble is, there are about seventeen and a half thousand possible combinations. All the planes are listening out on the same wavelength, so we can't try twenty or thirty different combinations at once—it has to be one at a time. At thirty seconds for each transmission, we'd need about five days to cover them all. We've got less than an hour and a half."

"We've also," Keppler said flatly, "only five minutes or so before the President gets here. There's just one idea I've got, but I need a little more information. Maybe General Franklin can supply it." He looked round at the other chiefs.

"What say we retire for a short while, take General Franklin with us?"

"Suits me," Admiral Maclellan said.

"And the Air Force," Steele broke in quickly. He wondered just what Keppler had up his sleeve. It had better be good, he thought. Because yet another six wings, fully armed, were now heading for their X points. Franklin hadn't wasted the time between the call from Omaha and the beginning of the meeting.

" ALABAMA ANGEL "

10.30 G.M.T.
Moscow: 1.30 p.m.
Washington : 5.30 a.m.

CLINT BROWN checked his flight instruments again. He had been checking them every thirty or forty seconds for the last ten minutes. At the moment he had very little to do, and so his mind prompted him to look for work, to do anything which would push the thought of Seattle and his fiancée into the background. It did not help that the rest of the crew were quiet and subdued. They too, he knew, would be finding it was not easy to put away unwelcome thoughts. A man can conquer his fear for himself more easily than his fear for those he loves. There was nothing to be done about it. He glanced at his wrist watch, checked the instruments again, looked out past the distant tip of the port wing into the icy blackness beyond. The hands on his watch moved round with agonising slowness to 10.31. He forced himself to wait until the exact second, then said, "O.K. Herman, you can arm up the hornets now."

"Roger," Goldsmith replied. He sounded eager, anxious to begin work.

Brown eased himself out of his seat and stood aside to let the engineer, Federov, climb into his place. It was normal practice for Federov to sit at the controls while the command pilot moved about the cabin.

Brown leaned over Stan Andersen's chart table, watching the navigator's busy fingers as he plotted information from the machines on to his chart, and fed back further information from the chart to the machines. Andersen looked up at Brown, smiled briefly. His face was set and drawn, but he at least was busy. "Still estimating 10.41, Stan?" Brown asked.

"Still 10.41. This wind's working out pretty good."

"Fine." Brown straightened up, went past Mellows, the radioman, who was sitting tense at his silent set. He gave Mellows a smile and a friendly pat on the shoulder as he went past. He was only a kid, Brown thought. But maybe that helped. Maybe he didn't grasp the full implications of what was happening.

As a matter of fact, Brown was wrong. Mellows realised quite well that by now the States had been hit. He was an only child, and his parents lived in Washington D. C. In his mind he knew that they were gone. All right, that was it, they were gone. It would be nice to be able to give way to his grief, but that was out. Right now he had the chance to avenge them, simply by doing his job. He would. He fondled the tune control of his radio, watched Brown stop by Goldsmith's fire control panel. He concenerated with all his determination on the set.

Goldsmith looked up at Brown. He nodded an acknowledgment of Brown's presence, then went back to his work. He had already pulled down each of the ten big switches ranged in banks of five at the top of the panel. Five weapons for the port firing tube, five for the starboard. Beneath each of the switches a red light glowed. As Brown watched intently the red lights flickered out one by one, and below them green lights flashed on in their place. The weapons were armed.

Goldsmith's hand now went to another row of switches, halfway down the panel. He selected the left hand switch of the port bank, and the left hand switch of the starboard. Again a red light glowed beneath each of the two switches.

In the rear of the fuselage two slim rockets, five feet long, slid quietly from a storage rack into a polished metal chute. Mechanical clamps pushed them smoothly along the chute to a point six feet short of the tail. Here the chute became a tube. The rockets vanished into the tube, leaving only the twelve firing ports of their motors in sight. Two hinged arms linked to the top of each tube slowly straightened. The tubes moved downwards, through an aperture formed by the sideways sliding of sections of the flooring. The rockets in their tubes hung a foot below the fuselage of *Alabama Angel*, vibrating slightly in the furious air blast, lethal now that the two safety plugs had been pulled out of warhead and motor as they dropped into firing position. On Goldsmith's panel the two red lights winked out and were replaced by green. The two missiles were primed and ready for firing.

Goldsmith looked up at Brown, said laconically, "Numbers one and six ready to go. Hope we don't need 'em." Then he turned to the radarscope that was linked in with the fire control system, adjusting the brilliance of the centre sweep.

Brown nodded. "Hope not," he agreed, and began to make his way back to his seat. On the way he passed Garcia and Minter, the ornance experts. Garcia looked worried, he noted, but Minter was his usual calm, unimaginative self.

He tapped Federov on the shoulder, took the engineer's place at the controls. A swift check of the dials showed everything normal, everything functioning smoothly. Glancing at his watch he saw that in another four minutes they would be turning on to the attack leg. In four minutes they would be sixty thousand feet above the imaginary dot on the Barents Sea which was exactly seventy-five degrees north, forty-five degrees east. From that point the bomber's track would be a straight line almost due south in heading, eight hundred and fifty nautical miles long, to the primary target. Brown wondered where along that line they would meet trouble—if they met it at all. And whether, if they met it, the defence systems built into the 52K's would take them safely through.

The modern bomber is an infinitely more complex machine than the crude Fortresses and Lancasters of World War II. It flies more than twice as fast and twice as high. With mid-air refuelling its range is virtually unlimited. But as the complexity and performance of the bomber have increased, so has the ability of its enemies to track it down and destroy it.

The 52K's were the last of their line. Their defence systems were the result of a triple alliance between the Boeing designers at Seattle, the weapons experts at Wright Field, and a specially formed electronics company in which both General Electric and Westinghouse had joined forces. Between them, they had made the 52K as nearly invulnerable to attack as any bomber could be.

The two main enemies of the bomber were guided missiles, whether launched from the ground or from another plane, and missiles fired from a supersonic fighter which were unguided but usually fired in salvoes to increase the chances of a hit.

Against the first of these enemies, the guided missile, the

52K deployed a whole battery of electronic counter-measures. As far as was known, the Russian missiles relied on radar in some form or other for their guidance systems. No doubt they were developing other forms of guidance, like the American and British infra-red missiles which homed on the radiations given off from jet engines. But it was thought that all operational missiles relied on radar.

The electronics company, on information supplied by the weapons teams at Wright Field, had designed a big electronic brain which would automatically sense the presence of a missile from its radar pulses. It would then determine the exact frequency of those pulses, assess the speed and track of the missile and beam out a series of pulses of its own. These would supply the enemy missile with false information, confuse its guidance system, and divert it from its target. In certain cases it would have the effect of causing the weapon to explode prematurely, in others of turning it back in its own track. In a whole series of tests against missiles of the same type the Russians were thought to be using, the brain had never failed to sense, and then to divert, an oncoming missile.

The Boeing people had looked at the size and weight of the electronic brain and its associated radar, shaken their heads, and declared it impossible to fit into the B-52. Then they had gone ahead and fitted it. The result was the 52K.

At the same time the electronic brain was being built into the 52, the conventional tail armament was removed. It no longer had the range for dealing with the second of the bomber's enemies—the supersonic fighter which would approach from the rear and loose off a salvo of rockets. These rockets were of the unguided type, and therefore impossible to divert electronically. If they were aimed right, nothing would stop them once they were launched. The solution was obvious. Kill the rocket carrying fighter before it could launch them.

The Air Force asked for, and got, a weapon which would do this. It had a long and involved set of initials for its name, but among SAC crews it was known as a hornet. The name was apt. A hornet sting is about as bad as you can get. A sting from the nuclear warhead—no bigger than a large grapefruit—of this hornet, would destroy anything within five hundred yards of the burst.

The hornet missiles were controlled initially by radar from the fire control system which Goldsmith operated. They were let slip as soon as a hostile fighter came within five miles range. In the first part of their flight they rode a beam from the bomber. At a range of a mile from the target their own infra-red guidance systems took over and homed them in. They were proximity fused to explode as soon as they were within two hundred yards of their targets. A series of tests had shown that when the missiles were released against a fighter five miles away, it was destroyed before it had penetrated to within two miles of the bomber. This was true even of fighters capable of twice the speed of sound in level flight.

So there it was, Brown thought. The two threats, the two counters. Now it remained to be seen just how the theory would work out in practice.

Andersen's voice broke in on him. "Two minutes to point A, captain. New course one seven eight. Estimating 12.05 at the primary."

"O.K. Setting it up now. What's the mid-point of our bomb time, Stan?"

"That's it, captain. Five after twelve. The earliest and latest times are one after and nine after."

"Right. Engineer, I'll want a fuel check after this turn. Work out the endurance from point A at this height and speed. Also at this height and twenty less speed. Give it to me in air miles."

"Right," Federov said. He took out his fuel analysis logs and his reckoner tables, and began to make the preliminary entries.

Brown opened his folder of orders again. "Radar?"

"Captain?" Lieutenant Owens spoke up clearly and confidently.

"Switch the brain to fully automatic as soon as we turn. Report to me when it's warmed up and functioning. I'll check the frequency search bands with you then. Stan, will the long range search help you on this leg?"

"Well," Andersen said, "we're a bit far away for the first fifteen minutes or so. Then we'll start picking up the southern half of Novaya Zemlya. You should be able to pick out Moller Bay a hundred and forty miles to port, Bill. About fifteen minutes after turning. After that I'll be interested in Kolguev Island and the Kanin Peninsula. Check with me when Moller Bay shows, huh?"

"Sure," Owens said. He turned to his main search radar, tuned it for maximum range, and selected the one hundred to two hundred mile range band. The radar would now concentrate exclusively on the area between two concentric circles, one a hundred and the other two hundred miles from their centre, which was *Alabama Angel*.

"Time to turn, Captain," Andersen's voice piped up.

"O.K. Stan, turning now." Brown watched as the port wing rose slowly, held its position steadily through the turn, and then dropped again. He checked the gyro heading, and said, "On course. Time to run to target?"

"Eighty-four minutes," Andersen said crisply.

"O.K." Brown leaned forward and turned the face of a count-down clock until the figure eight-four showed in the boldly framed datum window. He pressed the start button, and the clock began to tick away the remaining seconds and minutes. He watched it until the eight-four had clicked out of view and eighty-three had replaced it.

One minute gone on the attack leg. Eighty-three to go. Eighty-three more minutes of waiting and wondering. After the attack it would be a little easier, perhaps. They could break radio silence to request instructions what base they were to head for. Those instructions might give a clue what sort of damage the States had taken. Might. Of course, the instructions would possibly be sent without any request, as general instructions to the wing. There might even be a re-call. He forced the thought away from him, rejecting it as utterly impossible. They were committed now. Some of the wing—those with targets assigned to them deep inside central Russia—were over Russian territory already. There would be no recall.

He ran over in his mind what he had done already, what remained to do. Lieutenant Owens, the radar officer, said, "Captain, she's warmed up now, everything functioning. I'm ready to set up the frequency bands."

"O.K. Bill. You call them as you set them. I'll check with my list." Brown turned the pages of the folder until he reached the sheet that detailed the frequency bands to be set up on the electronic brain for this target and route. He checked off the bands as Owens called them, then said finally, "Right. Let me know immediately if you suspect any malfunctioning. If I'm speaking, break in on me. You understand?"

"Sure," Owens said. "I'll do that."

Brown turned to the very last page in the folder. He looked at the count-down clock for a moment. God, had only two more minutes gone by? How long were the other eighty-one going to seem? He thought back rapidly to the

checks he had made. Gunnery, navigation, radar, fuel. Fuel?
"Any idea on endurance yet, Federov?"

"I have the answer at this height and speed, Captain. Gives
you five thousand two hundred from the A point. I'm still
working on the other one."

"Thanks, Federov." Brown relaxed. He was two hundred
over the safety limit for this particular target. Allowing for
adverse winds, and extra fuel used in changes of altitude
which might be forced on a bomber for tactical reasons as it
approached its target, plan R called for *Alabama Angel* to
have the equivalent of five thousand air miles in the tanks at
the A point. He had a small margin to play with.

He glanced again at the count-down clock. It was showing
eightly. Perhaps he thought, even now, there would be
something which would. . . . The eighty clicked implacably
into seventy-nine. He said, "Garcia, Minter."

The two of them replied together, Garcia's voice blending
with the deeper notes of Minter's.

Brown took a deep breath. "Let's get to work," he said.
"Number one first. Arm and fuse for air burst at twenty
thousand. I'll check the stages with you."

Garcia said quietly, "Request release trigger for number
one."

"Releasing." Brown jerked down a switch on the instrument panel, held it down while he thumbed a button on the
left side of the panel with his other hand.

"I have it," Garcia said.

Brown let the switch flip up, took his thumb from the
button. The crew listened quietly to the preparations. And
Alabama Angel continued to push ten effortless miles behind her each minute on the way to the primary target.

SONORA, TEXAS

10.40 G.M.T.
Moscow: 1.40 p.m.
Washington: 5.40 a.m.

"SIT DOWN, Paul," Brigadier General Quinten said easily. He waved his hand to a comfortable chair in front of the desk.

Paul Howard looked carefully at the general as he sat down. He noted the haggard face, and the small twitch in the cheek under the right eye. But he also saw that the general's right hand was steady. And that was the hand holding the point four five pistol the general had produced, as if by magic, as soon as he heard Howard's first few words.

Quinten lit a cigarette. "So you've got on to it," he said. "How did you know?"

"Combination of things," Howard said slowly. "Mostly, the question of a bell ringing. It was there in back of my mind all the time, but it took a while to register. General, that red line phone makes a hell of a noise when it rings. Earlier on, when I came into this office and found you already speaking on that phone, I knew there was something missing. I didn't know just what. But a few minutes ago I realised it. *I hadn't heard the bell.* If it had rung, I'd have heard it for sure. So I began to get the idea you'd made the call to SAC yourself, strictly for my benefit." He paused, waiting for some positive reaction from Quinten.

But Quinten was not disturbed. "So far you're adding things up right," he said lightly. "I'm not going to quarrel with your conclusions. Go on from there."

"Well, sir, then I got to thinking about the second call,

the one that came through while I was talking to you. You said something like, 'I hear you. All right.' Something like that. It was just what you would have said if you'd picked up the phone for the first call and asked the operator at SAC to check your line. Anyway, I switched my radio on. The miniature one I keep in my desk. All the stations were transmitting normally, even the small local outfits."

"So?"

"So you'd said we were at warning red. That means air attack imminent. In that case all the small stations would have shut down. The networks would have shifted over to the Conelrad stations. That hadn't happened. It was then I realised."

"I see," Quinten murmured. "Paul, I was going to tell you anyway. I'd already told SAC, when I sent you to fetch the security officer, because it's too late for anyone to do anything about it now."

Howard lit a cigarette. He noticed the general had put the pistol down on the desk. But it was within easy reach of his right hand. He remembered one of the general's hobbies was pistol and small-bore rifle shooting. He relaxed. "I don't see how it's too late. SAC can recall the wing," he said.

"No, they can't. You weren't at the briefiing, were you?"

"You know I wasn't."

"So you don't know the three letter group I gave the wing, for setting on the CRM 114 after they received their attack orders?"

"No, I don't."

"Neither," Quinten said calmly, "does anyone at SAC."

"But the letters are pushed out by SAC," Howard protested, his voice rising slightly. "They're bound to know."

Quinten shook his head. "Paul, there are some things about SAC operations you don't know, and neither does any officer under base commander or deputy commander level. SAC supplies the general code group, sure. But the group for plan R is originated by the base commander himself. There's a good reason for it. We've learned a lot about the nature of Communism and its adherents. We also know we are liable to be attacked at any time. All right, suppose a sudden attack knocked out all our bases except this one. Suppose someone in high places knows the general code group of the day. Someone who is a Communist, or a fellow traveller."

"That isn't even a possibility," Howard said angrily.

"You're wrong, Paul. It *is* a possibility. In a world which can construct an H-bomb and put up its own artificial moons, even contemplate a break-out into space, nothing is impossible. *Nothing.* Oh, I agree the possibility is very slight, but it exists. Anyway, suppose things happened as I said. I get my planes into the air. But they aren't going to be much good if the enemy can get through to them and turn them back, or maybe divert them to a base where they can be caught on the ground a few minutes after landing. Plan R takes care of that. We've come a long way since Pearl Harbour. That taught us a lesson we've never forgotten, and the results of that lesson are written into plan R."

Howard shifted in his chair. Suddenly it was all very clear to him. He remembered how Majors Bailey and Hudson had asked permission to go on a hunting trip. The general had agreed immediately. Come to think, he was almost sure the general had suggested it. Bailey and Hudson had been at the briefing. Apart from the crews of the wing, and the general himself, they were the only officers who had.

"That's why you sent Bailey and Hudson off?" he asked.

Quinten frowned. For the past fifteen minutes the pain in his head had subsided to a dull throb. Now suddenly, it was again hot and active, clawing at his brain like a wild thing. He said quietly, "I don't know. Certainly, in the couple of minutes before the boys reached their X points, it was one of the factors influenced me to send them on in. That, and the news about the I.C.B.M. site, and the fact we were running a NORAD exercise so I knew our defences would be alert. You were standing in as deputy, which helped a lot. Colonel England would have smelled a rat immediately I mentioned plan R."

"I don't see why."

"You're forgetting that plan R was drawn up to take account of special circumstances," Quinten said gently. "To enable a base commander to act when central command had gone. It would never have been pushed out by SAC."

Howard stubbed out his cigarette in the ash receptacle built into the arm of the chair. "So now what happens?"

"Go and stand by the window, Paul. Listen very carefully."

Howard walked across to the window. He heard nothing. Then he pressed his ear against the thick glass, and felt it vibrating. Very faintly he heard a distant rumble, like thunder over the horizon of a summer's day.

"You hear anything?"

Howard turned to face him. "A low rumble," he said. "The kind of noise you hear when a wing goes off, if you're a long way away. That what you mean?"

Quinten nodded. "Exactly. Does it answer your question?"

Howard shook his head slowly. "I don't get it," he said. "I just don't understand what's happening."

"Sit down again." Quinten held the pistol loosely while Howard walked across the room, then replaced it on the desk as Howard sank into a chair. "Take your time to think about it, Paul. Tell me why you think a SAC wing is going off somewhere. You're graduated from the National War College, you know all the theory. Now work out the real thing."

Howard lit another cigarette. In the quiet lecture rooms of the War College it was easy. There was the problem, apply the tools of your training and natural brainpower to it, bingo —there was the solution. But that was when you were dealing with power in terms of paper symbols. The low rumble he had heard in the distance—was it from Sanderson? or Austin? or Uvalde?—was the real thing. It was power in terms of eight jet engines pushing out twelve thousand pounds of thrust each. It was power in terms of bombs with an explosive potential equivalent to fifteen million tons of T.N.T. Real power. Naked, frightening, unimaginable power.

"Well?" Quinten asked.

"General, I just don't know. I can't seem to figure things out. You've told SAC what you've done. Let's start from that. Would they know you've used plan R?"

"They'd know. Reception of the signals would tell them."

"All right, then they know they can't stop the eight forty-third. That means an attack will be made on Russia. Obviously, there'll be a counter-blow. So they have to get the other wings off the ground to make sure they aren't destroyed."

"Why would they want to do that?" Quinten asked. His tone was deceptively mild.

"Well, obviously they wouldn't want them destroyed if they could help it."

"Why?" Quinten pursued the question inexorably. "Think it through, Paul. You know the answer all right."

And suddenly Howard did know. Suddenly he saw the logical end of Quinten's action. Why bother to preserve the SAC wings *if they weren't going to be used?* He said slowly, "General, it seems to me they're planning to follow the eight forty-third in. Morally, we're already in the wrong, so therefore . . ."

Quinten broke in quickly. "I'd argue that. But let it go for the moment."

"Morally we're already in the wrong," Howard repeated stubbornly. "But are there degrees of morality in terms of the power locked up in those planes? Does it make any great deal of difference whether you kill thirty millions or sixty millions? Well, it seems to me it makes this difference. If they follow the eight forty-third in, they'll kill an extra thirty millions. I'm just guessing at the figures, of course. But that extra thirty millions will be in Russia. If they don't, then it's possible the Russians will kill thirty millions, here in America. Because of your action, they're faced with a choice of killing an extra number of Russians or letting the Russians kill an equal number of Americans. They're realists, they're bound to choose the first alternative. And that's why the SAC wings are going off." Suddenly he pushed back his chair. His face was very white. "Why in hell did you do it?" he shouted. "Why? For God's sake, why?"

"Sit down, Paul." Quinten's voice cracked sharply across the room. He brought the pistol up until it pointed at Howard. "Sit down, and cool off. I'm going to tell you why, later. I'm going to tell you what convinced me it was not only the expedient but also the moral thing to do. When you've heard me out, you'll be convinced too."

"No," Howard said firmly. "You may be able to convince me it was expedient. Never moral."

Quinten looked at him curiously. Howard's face was still a livid white, his fingers trembling as he crushed out his cigarette and immediately lit another. He was shocked, Quinten thought, by the sudden realisation. Yet he should not have been. No-one who had ever toted the actual bombs round the sky should have been shocked when he realised the bombs were going to be used. But undoubtedly Howard was shocked. Just as the crews of the bombers were shocked, probably, when they received the attack orders. It was another example of the way the mind will push the unpleasant things into the background. Like the envelope you fail to open because you know it contains a bill you can't really afford to pay. Like the politicians who manage to convince themselves during face-to-face meetings that the other man is friendly, when they know that yesterday he attacked them bitterly, and will probably do so again tomorrow.

Howard's cheeks were slowly returning to their normal, healthy colour. Quinten wondered what it was like to feel young, and strong, and free from pain. It had been so long, he had almost forgotten. He said, "Paul, you can think what you like of me, and so can the rest of the world. I know that what I've done is right. Do you remember what Clemenceau once said about war?"

"No, I don't." Howard's voice was almost normal again.

"He said war was too important a matter to be left to generals. At the moment he said it, he was probably right. But now it's swung the other way. When a war can be won and lost an hour after it starts, then war is too important to be left to politicians. The Russians know it. And they also know we don't work things that way. That's why, in a couple of hours from now, they'll have lost. There'll be no more threats from them. In a few hours the whole shape of the world will be changed. Remember what they did to Hungary back in '56? They won't be able to do that again, not ever."

"That's expediency. Morally, what you've done is still wrong."

"Well," Quinten said, "Maybe." He suddenly felt very thirsty. He picked up the gun from the desk, walked over to the water cooler by the window, and drank two full cups of water. Then he went back to his desk.

"Paul," he said. "You're going to be a part of the new

world. I'm not. I know quite well what history will have to say about my action. In two hundred years they'll have forgotten all about the menace of Communism. If you don't believe me, just think how soon we've forgotten what we once felt about Germany. And Japan. I'll just be remembered as a butcher, a man who wantonly slaughtered millions of innocent people. Tell me—do you really think I'm that kind of man? Do you really think I can take an action which will snuff out millions of lives with as little compunction as I'd squash a fly?"

"Well, no I don't. At least," Howard paused and looked deliberately at Quinten, "I didn't up to now. Now I'm not sure."

"You can be," Quinten said quietly. "A few hours from now I'll be dead. I happen to believe in a life after this one, so I believe I will have to answer for what I've done. I think I can."

Howard looked at him with fresh interest. "I don't quite follow. If the rest of SAC are going in after the eight forty-third, we're bound to win. It's possible we won't be hit at all in this country. Why should you be dead?"

Quinten tapped a cigarette on the desk carefully, placed it between his lips, and struck a match. Then he blew the match out without lighting the cigarette. "Because if I let myself live it would be as a lunatic. The human mind could never withstand a traumatic experience as violent as the killing of all those millions of people. I'm going to tell you a little of why I did this. But first, let me ask you another question. When you heard that wing going off in the distance the sound was something monstrous, something inhuman and dreadful to you. Right?"

"Right."

"No, Paul. There was nothing monstrous about it. You

know what that sound meant? I'll tell you. It meant peace on earth."

THE PENTAGON

10.45 G.M.T.
Moscow: 1.45 p.m.
Washington: 5.45 a.m.

"THERE ARE only two alternatives," General Steele said. He paused and looked round the long table. The President, at the head of the table, was inclining slightly forward to listen. The Secretaries of State and Defence were at his right and left hand respectively, and between them and the service chiefs the intervening seats were occupied by the heads of Atomic Energy Commission, Central Intelligence Agency, Civil Defence, and F.B.I.. It was almost, but not quite, a full meeting of the National Security Council. Only two or three members were missing, and they were out of Washington.

"The first of these," Steele went on, "seems at this moment to be impossible of fulfilment. It is that the eight forty-third wing be recalled. I am not going to suggest there is not the slightest chance of doing this. We may, by some lucky break, hit on the right letter combinations. But the odds against that, in the time remaining to us, are in the order of a hundred to one. For the moment anyway.

"I use the expression 'for the moment', because General

Keppler has suggested a way in which we might be able to establish personal contact with the commander at Sonora —a contact which so far he has refused to prolong beyond his bald statement that the wing were attacking on his personal orders. I will revert to this suggestion after examining the second of the alternatives."

"One moment," the President broke in. "I think I'd like to hear about it before you pass on to the second alternative."

"Very well, sir. It so happens the Seventy Fourth Infantry Division are on tactical dispersal training in the immediate vicinity of Sonora. General Keppler has suggested they be ordered to penetrate Sonora Base, to establish contact with the commander and with any other officer who was present when the crews were briefed. Only those officers would know the code group which the commander gave the crews at the briefing."

"Would it be necessary to use force to achieve this, er, penetration?"

Steele glanced at Franklin, who was standing in the group surrounding the table, and motioned him forward. "General Franklin, the commander of SAC, is here, Mr. President. With your permission, he's the best man to answer that question."

The President nodded. "Well, Franklin? Would force be necessary?"

"Most certainly," Franklin said bluntly. "I've been thinking what I'd have done in Quinten's place. I'd know that the attack orders would be monitored, so my first concern would have been to seal off the base. I feel sure Quinten has brought the base to warning red conditions, which means all non-combatants are now below ground, and the defence teams will be in their battle positions. No doubt he has instructed them to fire on anyone or anything that tries to penetrate the base unless he personally orders them not to.

Any force which tried to penetrate would surely come under fire. There would be heavy casualties on both sides."

General Keppler said pleasantly, "Not so many as you may think. With respect to your defence teams, General, they're not infantry. They're airmen and technicians with a smattering of training in the operation of defensive weapons. The seventy-fourth is one of our Ranger divisions. They'll brush the defence aside without too much trouble."

The President saw Franklin's face slowly darken. In the few weeks he had been President he had already experienced one major inter-service row and three or four minor squabbles. Now the foundations of yet another dispute were being laid for the future. If there was going to be a future, he thought grimly. Before Franklin could reply he intervened. "How long before they can move in, General Keppler?"

An aide stepped forward and whispered to Keppler. The burly general smiled. "They've got there pretty fast, Mr. President. The second battalion is in position five hundred yards off two sides of the fencing now." He looked at Franklin, grinned, and carefully laid an inch of ash from his cigar in one of the massive glass ashtrays which were ranked down the middle of the table.

The President did not miss the by-play between Keppler and Franklin. He noted it, but it did not engage any large part of his conscious attention. He was considering the situation. Somewhere on that base there must be an officer who knew the code group. Perhaps the commander himself would pull back when he heard what the President had to tell him. Inevitably, there would be casualties. Possibly heavy casualties, though Keppler should know the capabilities of his troops. But the situation was such that casualties must be accepted. The few would have to suffer for the sake of the many. He made his decision.

"Send them in," he said quietly. "I want the minimum in

casualties, but they are not to let the necessity of inflicting casualties deter them from taking the commander alive at the earliest possible time. Instruct the battalion commander he is to institute an immediate search for any officers who were present at the briefing."

Keppler turned in his chair. The aide stepped forward, listened, then turned and hurried from the room.

"Now, General Steele," the President said. "Please continue."

The Air Force Chief of Staff began to speak again. "The Joint Chiefs have come to the conclusion that the only course open to us is to follow up Quinten's action. That is the second of the alternatives. It is a fact, Mr. President, that the eight forty-third will probably be able to hit each of the priority one targets. We think, furthermore, they will take out these targets before the Russians are able to get any effective retaliatory force off the ground. Provided the eight forty-third is followed by a sufficiently strong attack, delivered by at least eight wings, the Russians will not be able to retaliate on the American continent at all. We cannot guarantee the integrity of targets in Western Europe, but we think there is a good chance the Russians will be so concerned in fighting off our attack and trying to scrap together resources for a counter they will probably not be able to mount an effective attack on those targets.

"We considered also the possibility of a retaliatory strike by submarines firing guided missiles from off our coasts. The Chief of Naval Operations is satisfied we can defeat this threat. Our main concern in the past has been the huge sea areas we have to cover to guard against attacks on the SAC bases in the South and South-west. But once our main attacks have been delivered, we can afford to abandon those bases. Our sea defences can then be concentrated on comparatively short and narrow belts of water opposite the

East and West coasts. We feel we can then ensure missiles from submarines will not hit our coastal and near-coastal cities.

"Our conclusions can be summarised thus. Accepting we cannot recall the bombers of the eight forty-third wing, there is an absolute military necessity to follow up their attack as hard and as fast as we can. Any other course of action will inevitably mean that we lose cities, and take casualties. Not just a few, but millions of them. In anticipation of your decision, ten SAC wings are already heading for their X points. They can put in their attack between two and seven hours after the eight forty-third. Mr. President, the Joint Chiefs unanimously recommend that a full scale attack on Soviet Russia be launched immediately."

"Concur," Admiral Maclellan said precisely.

"Concur," Keppler growled.

The President stood up abruptly. He paced down the long room to where the semi-circle of chairs faced the big wall maps. He watched as the plotters neatly drew intersecting lines across the tracks of the target-bound bombers. Each little intersection represented another five minute advance towards the target, based on the flight plan estimates. He sighed.

It was so simple. An elementary exercise in military theory. The Joint Chiefs were professionals, and their solution was undoubtedly the right one. He continued to gaze at the central map.

Slowly the officers and civilians who had been sitting at the big table drifted down to group themselves behind him. In a time of national emergency, the President stands at the very apex of the councils of power. Through him must flow the proposals and counter-proposals on all matters affecting the national security. From him must come the ultimate policy decisions. That is the constitution.

He stood silent for a full two minutes in front of the central map. He tried to think himself into the position of his opposite number in the Kremlin. All his life, even when at a comparatively late age he had found himself sucked into the hurly burly of politics, he had read and admired the great Russian novelists. Now he bent the knowledge he had acquired from them of the Russian character into an attempt to solve the one great dilemma with which he was faced. He did not believe the character of a people can change overnight, whatever change of government there might have been. He thought of the Russian peasant; stubborn, obstinate, accustomed to suffering and perhaps even welcoming it. Latent in all the Slavs, he thought, is the urge for self destruction, the mute acceptance of nemesis once nemesis is seen to be at hand.

He turned abruptly to the waiting group. "Gentlemen," he said, "we're not going to do it." His tone was crisp and authoritative. "General Steele."

"Mr. President?"

"Recall the SAC wings. Keep them airborne if you feel it necessary for their safety, but they are not to proceed to their X points without direct authority from me."

Steele turned away abruptly. He moved over to Franklin. "You heard, Keith," he said. "Bring them on back." He dropped his voice a little. "But not too far. Arrange for tankers to meet them not more than four hours from their targets. Prepare them to stay airborne just as long as is necessary. If they get hungry, all right they get hungry. But I want them kept airborne, and I want them kept topped with fuel. I still think they're going to be needed."

"I know they will," Franklin said. It was a definite statement of fact. Like Quinten, Franklin had no great opinion of politicians, especially when they interfered with the weapon he had helped to forge. But Franklin was not a sick man. More important, he had not the same freedom of action Quinten had. He went away to give out the orders. Steele turned back to the group around the President.

The President spoke directly to him. "General Steele, you think my decision is madness." It was phrased as a statement, but everyone in the group took it as a question.

Steele looked at the President. Never in his life had he evaded the truth when asked for his opinion. He did not propose to begin now. He said, "Sir, so far as I can see, it is madness. You have overlooked that if we succeed in recalling the eight forty-third, we can easily recall the other wings. If we do not succeed those wings are going to be necessary. I will go further than that. Not only will they be necessary, they will stand between life and death for millions of people in this country."

The President smiled. "Thank you, General. Let me assure you I have not taken the decision lightly."

Well, Steele thought, *they would see.* Meanwhile, he could rely on Franklin holding the wings where they could be sent in to their targets with the minimum delay.

The President looked at the map again. He gazed particularly at the heavy brown shading of the Urals. He said, "Get me Moscow. I want to speak to the Marshal himself. No-one else will do."

The senior of the two presidential aides said nervously, "Mr. President, it's possible the Marshal will not be available."

"Tell him this," the President said, his words coming slowly and distinctly. "Tell him in an hour and a quarter from now his major cities, including Moscow, will be taken out. He'll be available."

"Taken out?" the aide queried.

"Taken out, destroyed, obliterated, phrase it how you like. The words don't matter. The cities and the people do." He paused, considering carefully what else there was to be said. "Tell him also," he continued very quietly, "I'm greatly afraid I won't be able to prevent it."

The aide hurried away. The President glanced at his watch. It was five minutes to six, Washington time. He turned briskly to the group. "Now gentlemen, things to be done. NORAD alerted. Steele?"

"It's been done, Mr. President."

"Good. The fleets at sea, Admiral Maclellan?"

"They've been alerted, sir."

"All right. I don't consider there is a need to evacuate the cities yet. Any threat against them won't develop for some time. Maybe," his voice was thoughtful, "for some considerable time. I'll need a complete communications system between this room and Moscow. At least a dozen independent outlets. The Russian Ambassador will be arriving shortly, and I want him brought right in with no unnecessary formalities. Yes, Keppler?"

Keppler flushed. He did not like bucking authority, but this was madness. Within minutes of entering the War Room the ambassador could not fail to assimilate the most vital of all defence secrets. "The communications system is easy, sir. We already have all the outlets here we need. It's just a question of hooking them to a radio net." He paused, not too sure just how far he should go. "About the Russian Ambassador," he began hesitantly.

"He enters on my personal orders." The President's voice was quiet, but firm. "Now I wish to talk to the Joint Chiefs in private."

Individuals broke away from the group and dispersed down the room. At the long table they merged into a group again, as though the table acted as a focal point, bringing them together to converse in low, excited voices. Twenty yards away, the President was talking to the three service officers.

"A few moments ago," he said, "I made a decision you

thought was military nonsense. As far as your information and your knowledge goes, I'll agree that it was. But I happen to know a little more than you.

"I'm now forced to let you into a secret which up to the present has been known only to the President himself and the Secretary of State. It was passed on personally to me by my predecessor when ill health finally forced him to relinquish the Presidency. In my opinion, the knowledge he had to bear contributed directly to the decline in his health, but that is by the way. There are reasons you have not been allowed to have this information. The most important of them is that once you have it, you will see than an all-out attack on Russia is futile. Obviously, that would affect your attitude to your duties, and that would have been fatal, for it would have encouraged the enemy to attack, in the knowledge that though our defences are strong, yet we would hesitate to use our powers of retaliation.

"General Steele, I can see you don't agree. Let me ask you a question. Could you, as Chief of Air Force, order an all-out attack on Russia if you knew that attack would inevitably mean the destruction of the United States?"

"Mr. President, the premises are false. If I ordered an all-out attack on Russia now, the United States would not be destroyed."

"You're wrong. Not only would the United States be destroyed, but all the rest of the world too. Not spectacularly, and not at once, but quite inevitably. Radio-activity, you will agree, can destroy life just as effectively as blast or heat?"

"In the long run," Steele said. "But the big bombs we're using aren't rigged that way. There's no reason the fall-out should exceed that of a small atomic explosion."

"And the Russians' bombs?"

"They don't affect the issue. If this attack goes through and is followed up, those bombs will never be delivered."

"Not on this country, no. But do they need to be delivered here? Now I am going to give you the information which was passed on to me by my predecessor. It is a quite simple idea, but if you look at it carefully you will see it really is the ultimate deterrent. You take a couple of dozen hydrogen devices. They don't need to be bombs, no airplane is going to be called on to carry them. You jacket those devices in cobalt, and you bury them in a convenient mountain range. They can be exploded at the press of a button. All of them. How long would you give human life on this earth after such an explosion?"

The President paused, looked at each of the three faces in turn. They were thoughtful, puzzled, perhaps a little frightened as discernment came to them. "The Atomic Energy Commission were given that question as a theoretical exercise. Their answer was this. That all life would cease in the northern hemisphere between eight and fourteen weeks after the explosion. The southern hemisphere would last longer, depending on the time of year. Five months at the minimum, ten at the maximum. There would be no escape from the radio-active cloud. It would enshroud the entire earth, and poison every living organism. It would retain its lethality for hundreds of years. It would mean the end of the world. Literally."

Admiral Maclellan shook his head. "But that would be suicide," he said slowly. "The nation or person who set off such an explosion would die with the rest."

"Exactly," the President said. "*But the rest would die.* Gentlemen, we have incontestable proof the Russians have buried at least twenty, maybe more, of these devices in the Urals. It is my belief, based on a lifetime's study of the Russian character in particular, and also the behaviour of dictators facing defeat in general, that if they see they are beaten they will not hesitate to fire those devices.

"Have you any doubt Hitler would indeed have brought the world down in flaming ruins if he had had the power to do so when Berlin was under siege? Fortunately, he did not have the power, he could only destroy himself. But notice that he did destroy himself, rather than endure defeat. In every dictatorship which is tottering, there is an urge towards destruction. Of self, if that only is possible. Of the world, if that is. Gentlemen, I am convinced if the eight forty-third wing carry out their mission, and with such success it is obvious to the Russians they have lost, then they will press the button. And if they do, within ten months from now our Earth will be as dead as the Moon.

" ALABAMA ANGEL "

10.55 G.M.T.
Moscow: 1.55 p.m.
Washington: 5.55 a.m.

"THAT DOES IT, Captain. Check main switch off." Garcia's voice indicated satisfaction and relief.

"Main switch off."

"Check bomb release link switch off."

"Bomb release link switch off," Lieutenant Engelbach said.

Brown looked at his watch. The first of the weapons had been armed in a little under nine minutes. Pretty good. The best time they had recorded in the synthetic trainer back at Sonora was eight minutes three seconds. But that was in a trainer, running the drill on a dummy bomb. It made a difference, a whole heap of difference, when the bomb was real and you were arming it for a real attack.

Brown thought he could use a cup of coffee. The arming up had been a big strain. There was no possibility of accidental detonation in the bomb bay. But there was a real possibility the bomb would not detonate at all when it was dropped if they slipped up on the drill. They had not slipped up. All the circuits glowed green. When the time came, the first weapon was ready.

He decided a cup of coffee would have to wait until the second bomb had been armed. "O. K., Garcia, what do you say. Let's get the time down on this one, huh? Then maybe a cup of coffee."

"Sure thing, Captain." Garcia sounded confident and cheerful. That was natural enough. He and Minter had just performed their duty competently and well. No matter just what the duty was, they had the satisfaction which comes to any man who has done a good job.

"Right. Number two, then. Arm and fuse for air burst at twenty-five thousand."

"Air burst, twenty-five. Release trigger primer for number two."

"Releasing." Again the drill with the switch on the right side of the panel, the button pressed simultaneously on the left side. Both controls had to be operated, and at the same time. If they were not, the trigger primer remained locked in its insulated steel container.

"I have it," Garcia said. Very delicately he removed the device from the container, whose side door had slid open when Brown operated the two controls. Minter bent over Garcia, and accepted the device from him.

The trigger primer contained no sort of nuclear charge. It was a simply a number of high explosive cartridges, wired in series for electric detonation. Its function was to hurl a certain mass of plutonium down a tube rather like a gun barrel into another mass. On their own, the two masses, were harmless. When flung violently together an uncontrolled reaction took place and an atomic explosion occurred. The plutonium triggers of the bombs carried by *Alabama Angel* were themselves several times as powerful as the atomic weapons which wrecked Hiroshima and Nagasaki.

Surrounding the atomic trigger was a core of tritium, hydrogen of triple weight, which when ignited by the atomic explosion burned hot enough and long enough to detonate the main charge of the bomb, made of deuterium. The deuterium charge gave each bomb the equivalent power of fifteen million tons of T.N.T.

The bombs were fifteen feet long and about six feet across at their widest part. They were roughly cylindrical in shape, with a short, blunt nose and stubby tail fins. They were not very good ballistically, but could be dropped with an average error of between a half and two thirds of a mile. Since everything within ten miles of ground zero would certainly be destroyed by the heat and blast effects alone, inaccuracies of that degree were quite acceptable.

Garcia slid back the cover of a fat steel tube. Minter very carefully fitted the primer into the tube, sliding the four raised flanges on its sides into the grooves cut for them on the inside of the tube. He pushed the device home, stood away, and let Garcia slide back and screw down the cover.

"Trigger primer in contact tube. Cover secured," Garcia reported.

"O.K.," Brown said. "Let her down." He glanced at his watch. Under three minutes so far. The boys were on the ball.

Minter pressed a button built into the side of the tube. The primer began its slow journey down the tube, the flanges sliding smoothly in the four grooves. When it reached the level of the cabin floor the thick lead wall at the bottom of the tube slid back, a tell tale indicator showing its movement to Garcia and Minter. The primer went down past the protective wall, which slid back into place as soon as it had passed. Ten seconds later, a green light on the arming panel showed that it was securely in position within the bomb.

Garcia said, "Primer in position. Contact tube sealed."

"O.K. Good going fellows. Check circuits."

Garcia and Minter worked rapidly, not getting in each other's way. They tested each of the sixteen leads to the firing cartridges. Then they checked bomb release leads, emergency circuit leads, radar altimeter and barometric fuse circuits. All were in order. They made the final formal check for cabin radiation. "Main switch off, Captain," Garcia said.

"Main switch off." Brown looked at his watch again as Garcia checked the bomb release link switch with Engelbach. Exactly eight minutes. "Men, you've earned some coffee. Eight minutes flat." He sounded very pleased.

Garcia grinned. Minter managed a fleeting, economical smile. "Coffee coming right up," Garcia said.

Brown looked at his count-down clock. Fifty-nine minutes to go. He accepted a cup of coffee from Garcia, sipped it. It was good and hot. "How long before we cross in, Stan?"

"We should cross in at eleven twenty-two. Sixteen minutes from now."

"O.K." Brown finished his coffee. "Speed working out all right?"

"I think so. Let you know a little later."

"All right, men. Combat ready. Have the pressurisation and emergency oxygen ready and set for full, Federov."

"Set for full, Captain."

"O.K. Everyone make sure your oxygen supply is linked to emergency as well as normal." Brown checked that his own supply was doubly connected. He wasn't anticipating trouble yet. That would come later, when the coastal radar had identified them as hostile and the defences had been alerted. He felt sure from what he knew about the Russian radar net on this coast they hadn't even picked up *Alabama Angel* yet. But it never hurt to be prepared. Maybe nothing would get through to hit the bomber. But if it did, and if the pressure cabin was perforated, then the emergency oxygen and the pressure breathing system linked to it would enable the crew to live while he took the bomber down below forty-six thousand feet, where breathing was possible without pressure systems.

Lieutenant Owens, radar officer, said, "You see Kolguev Island yet, Stan?"

"I don't think so," Andersen replied. He adjusted the brilliance control of his radarscope, which was a repeater fed from Owens' scope.

"11 o'clock, about a hundred and thirty." Owens' attention was suddenly drawn to his other scope. Two flashes of light had appeared where no flashes should be. There they were again. "Holy cow!" he yelled. "Missiles, captain. Sixty miles off, heading in fast from twelve o'clock. Steady track, they look like beam riders."

"Roger, keep watching them." Brown's voice was calm and assured. Well, they'd soon know if the Wright Field boys had been on the ball. He reached forward and took the controls out of auto-pilot. Strangely, he felt not in the least scared. They were committed. The missiles were on their way. Maybe the brain could divert them, maybe not. There was nothing he could do about it.

"Forty-five," Owens said. His voice was higher pitched than usual, but he was not conscious of that. "Still coming straight and fast."

"Any idea on speed?"

"Between two and three thousand."

"Keep watching. Call them every five miles."

"Roger. Thirty-five. Still straight."

The crew waited silently. They too accepted the fact there was nothing they could do. Goldsmith's hornets were no use against things travelling at that speed. They would have to sweat it out. Mellows concentrated on his set. Federov made a few meaningless notations on his fuel analysis sheet. Minter was apparently unmoved, but Garcia found himself repeating words he had not used since he was a boy. He was unaware that it was a simple prayer.

"Thirty. Still twelve o'clock. Speed around two thousand six hundred."

Brown became conscious he was tightening his grip on the controls. He eased it off. The palms of his hand were wet and cold.

"Twenty-five. Still straight."

Stan Andersen completed another series of calculations. They were starting to run behind time. He heard Owens call the missiles at twenty miles. They'd have to beef up the power a little. Another two or three hundred revolutions would be enough. But that could wait until after. After? He shrugged, and returned to the private world of abstruse calculations and meticulously accurate plotting that was his own.

"Fifteen. Still straight."

Brown felt a sudden irritation on his forearms, the kind of irritation that comes with a bad dose of prickly heat. It had to be soon now. One way or the other.

"Ten miles, still heading straight. Hey, wait a minute, they're splitting up. One's showing ten o'clock now, going away. That won't hit us. The other's coming into five. Five now, still coming. Still twelve o'clock, maybe a little to starboard, it's swinging away. Four miles, two o'clock, three miles, three o'clock, it's going past to the starboard. They've gone, Captain, both of them."

Brown grinned. He had caught a glimpse of the missile that passed them to starboard, seen it momentarily as a bright red streak across the sky. "Well, fellows, that's it. Let's not relax, but I guess we can all feel a little happier. The brain works," he said.

"Man, I would like to do something for the guy dreamed up that brain. For him I would do anything. But anything." Goldsmith's voice was happy and relieved.

"Even make him a present of your little black book, hey Herman?" Andersen asked quietly.

"Well, maybe not quite that much. But . . ."

Owens broke in on Goldsmith. "Two more, Captain. Coming in from twelve o'clock like the last pair. Same speed. And a third, ten miles behind the other two. Fainter blip, probably a bit smaller. Not so fast, either."

"O.K. Call them." Brown wondered why they were meeting missiles so far out. He shrugged. It didn't matter much so long as they weren't hitting.

The crew listened to Owens call the ranges and bearings. But this time the tension was gone. They had seen that the brain worked, and they had faith in it now.

Andersen requested and got an engine adjustment to push up the speed another ten. He began to work on a new series of calculations. He heard Owens call the two missiles in to ten miles, and again they were diverted, both of them to port.

The third missile was slower than the other two. It was still fast, of course, but under two thousand. Owens found he had plenty of time to compute its speed. He worked it out at eighteen hundred and fifty, and passed the information to Brown.

Brown said, "O.K. Call it at ten."

"Coming up to ten now. Wonder which way this one will go. Eight miles now, still coming steady. Six, no change.

There she goes, out to two o'clock now. Four miles. Four o'clock, three miles. Three miles! Captain," his voice was loud and high, "this one's turning in on us. Five o'clock, two miles. Six o'clock, one mile. My God, it's . . ."

Brown never heard the rest of the message It was drowned out by the explosion.

SONORA, TEXAS

11.00 G.M.T.
Moscow: 2 p.m.
Washington: 6 a.m.

"ONLY AN HOUR to go for some of them," Quinten said quietly. He smiled tiredly at Major Howard. "Paul, you're about as stubborn as a Missouri mule. You understand the nature of this thing we've been fighting. You understand that we *have* been fighting although we're officially at peace. It seems the only thing you can't understand is we've finally been given a chance of winning the fight."

Howard shrugged. "There are lots of people wouldn't agree about the fighting part. At least, they haven't slung any nuclear weapons at us."

"You think they wouldn't?"

"I can only repeat they haven't."

"Not yet," Quinten said slowly. "Not yet. Because they can't be sure of winning, yet. But on the day they are sure, they'll sling them. They've spent long enough planning for it."

"Well, I don't know. Whenever we've met them firmly, they've pulled back. I agree we had to be as strong as they were, and show them we were prepared to use our strength. But they've always pulled back. I take that to mean our policy's paid off."

"Policy!" Quinten said bitterly. "What policy? Did it rescue Hungary? Or Poland? Did it stop them taking over the majority of people in the Far East? Or keep them out of the Mediterranean? Have you ever really thought what our policy is?"

"Well," Howard said, "sure I have. I guess everyone knows it's basically a policy of containment. We don't like them, but we have to admit they exist, we have to live in the same world with them. All right, let's find a way of doing it, while at the same time keeping our guard up and letting them know we're ready for them. That's been our policy."

Quinten looked at him thoughtfully. "And how have we pushed that policy through?"

"Economic aid to the under developed countries. Military aid to Europe. Military strength of our own sufficient to deter any large scale aggression. In the main, it's worked out."

"You think so? Listen, Paul, you don't kid yourself. It's failed. It's failed economically. We poured billions out in aid. Russia watched us doing it, and smiled. In a lot of countries we managed effectively to destroy colonialism. But we didn't supply a political dynamic sufficiently strong to hold off the Communists as well as replace the colonial systems we helped to end. Very often—as in China—the money and goods we sent simply helped to make the rich much richer, the poor much poorer. Because we failed to appreciate that while big business can maybe help to run a highly developed and educated country, it doesn't mean a thing to the peasants of a backward country.

"So what happened? We preached plenty for all in a few

years. The Communists simply promised an extra bowl of rice a day immediately the people had overthrown their rulers. An extra bowl of rice can be understood simply. A favourable economic balance created through a hydro-electric scheme that will take six years to complete, cannot. All right, so they'd have got their hydro-electric scheme, and they never have got their extra bowl of rice. So what? The peasants live at starvation level, like they've always lived. If they grumble, they're shot. There are plenty of them to spare, and now the Communists have taken over there's an efficient system of control and suppression. Short of a major war, their rulers can never be deposed. Since the war a dozen countries have gone Communist. Name me one that's shaken off Communism."

Howard said, "General, I realise that. But I think it's an over-simplification of the issue." He noticed that Quinten was flushed, and there were beads of sweat on his forehead.

"I know. But it's a fair assessment of what's happened. We've failed militarily, too, because we were outguessed all along the line. When we were thinking in terms of A-bombs, Russia thought in terms of bayonets. There were plenty of those available. They implemented the first part of her plan. Unless I'm wrong, the second part was due to be implemented very soon now.

"You see, the Russians had one tremendous advantage. They could set a definite date when they would launch their final bid for world domination. In 1945, that date was twenty or more years off. They planned accordingly. They had bayonet power, but little else. All right, let bayonet power gain as much as it could, then hold what it had gained until the time came for the final blow. They figured correctly that the Western countries—particularly ourselves and the British—were tired of war. We wouldn't fight a major war over the Balkans, or the Baltic States, or even China. Those countries went under. They had minor setbacks. In Korea, for example. But the first part of the plan succeeded, and bayonet powed did it for them. When bayonet power was no longer effective, they called a halt until they could replace it with something else. By that time, they didn't think it would be too long in coming.

"The German rocket experts gave them their first breakthrough. A handful of spies gave them their second. Their planners decided that war would be possible from about 1960. Maybe a little earlier if they skipped a generation of weapons. They did just that. Do you follow me?'

"Not altogether," Howard said. "They aren't the kind of people to take military risks. Why should they risk skipping a generation of weapons?"

"No risk," Quinten said sharply. "No risk at all. We've told them loudly enough and often enough we'll never attack them first. The Rockefeller report drew attention to that, as well as the enormous advantage they gain from it. Remember what it said in 1958? That unless present trends are reversed, the world balance of power will shift in favour of the Soviet bloc. It also said the Soviet's greatest advantage is that the Communists, by their very nature, are ready to strike the first blow. They need only prepare for the way they intend to fight. On the other hand, we must be on the defensive and gear our planning and procurement against any possible form of attack at any possible time. When the first two Russian satellites went into orbit the writing was on the wall. They passed us."

"Ours didn't lag by too much. A matter of months only."

"But months are important. I want you to understand that, Paul. As the destructive potential of weapons has increased, so the margin of retaliatory time has decreased. Russian I.C.B.M. sites fully operational even two days before their counterparts over here, can win the war. That's where the Russian planning has been so good."

"Not with some of SAC airborne, it's not so good."

"I don't agree. Sure they'll get hit, but how hard? Understand, I don't think the margin of superiority will rest with them long. Maybe two or three months while their sites are operational and ours are not. The short period still to run before NORAD can effectively track their missiles coming in and give us time to fire off ours and get SAC off the ground. But that's what they've planned for. Even a two week magin of superiority would be enough. Maybe two hours. That's why war's too important to be left to the politicians now."

Howard lit a cigarette. He pondered on what Quinten had been saying. Militarily, it made sense. If you could produce a heavy enough initial blow, the chances were you would win. Your weapons had enough sheer brute power in them to swamp opposition. But who could say those weapons would be used? Where did the strictly military line of capability end, and the political line of probability start? He said, "So they could hit us, and they could take us out. If we accept that, we still have to ask whether they'd do it. And if they would, then why."

"First, yes they would," Quinten said crisply. "And second, because only then can they achieve world domination. That's their real purpose. Nationally speaking, it's nothing new. Czarist Russia was essentially expansionist. And the nature of a people doesn't change overnight, even if the politicians can't see it that way. They're after nothing less than world domination. For the first time they have the chance to achieve it militarily. Their lead in rockets has given them the chance, but it won't last very long. You think they'll let it slip away from them? From sentiment, maybe? Or humanitarian feelings? Or a belief it's wrong to kill? You really think that?"

Howard shifted uncomfortably. Damn it, Quinten was utterly convincing. Yet he knew the reasoning was wrong somewhere. There had to be a fallacy. If you are dedicated to the principle of non-aggression, you cannot just discard the principle on a theoretical assumption. He said, "General, you forget one thing. We've sworn to defend a way of life that gives every man the right to live without fear of attack. I agree with lots of what you say about Russia, and the Russian leaders. But you won't justify killing millions of ordinary people, who just want to live their lives, because you have an idea their leaders are going to attack us. That way you put us in their class. You put us among the monsters, the animals in the jungle."

"I'm glad you mentioned that. But remember the jungle isn't of our making. You know, when I was a kid I used to read a lot. Anything I could lay my hands on, we didn't have too much money for books in my house. I had nine or ten books which were my own, and I read them over and over. Among them was the Jungle Book. Rudyard Kipling. You ever read it?"

"I don't think so."

"You should. In particular, read the story of the little mongoose called Rikki-tikki-tavi, because of the noise he made, and how he was taken into a house as a pet after the river floods swept him out of his mother's nest. In the garden of the house live a couple of cobras, and pretty soon the mongoose kills the male cobra, because it's laying for the man of the house. But the female cobra is left. And she's got a clutch of eggs will produce a few dozen young cobras. She knows she can't rule the roost in the garden while Rikki's around, so she decides he has to go. She says so, and she means it.

"The little mongoose weighs up the odds. He can handle the cobra if she comes at him. He just has to watch his step, and be ready for her any time. But the eggs hatching out are something else. Once they're hatched and the young cobras become dangerous—operational you might call it—he's gone. He can't handle that many at once, they'll be too strong for him.

"So he waits his chance, and when the female cobra is causing mischief somewhere else, he breaks those eggs. The cobras inside the shells aren't dangerous to him—yet. But it's just a question of time, then they will be. So he kills them. He doesn't have to ask for proof—his instinct tells him a mongoose doesn't live with a snake. He kills the snakes, or the snakes kill him. So he acts, and he lives. He destroys the eggs, and then he destroys the mother cobra. He's safe, and the people in the house are safe. They can live their lives in peace. It's a good story, Paul, and a good analogy too."

"You really think so?"

"I really think so. I've forgotten your record of service. Have you ever had personal contact with them?"

"No," Howard shook his head. "Not personal."

Quinten looked levelly at him. "I have," he said, "just a few times. One was in Austria. Officially, the war had been over a few days. But the Russian columns were still moving forward. I watched the Mongolian troops enjoying themselves. By that I mean raping women. By women I mean any female they could lay their hands on between six and sixty. All right, they were animals, they knew no better. But their officers did, and they refused to intervene. That, I saw personally. There was nothing we could do about it. We had a handful of officers and men there, and they had several divisions. I began to hate them then.

"In Berlin, I went to a party one night. A Russian officer got drunk. Well, that wasn't unusual, but this one got drunker than most. He took me aside. He said he liked me personally, but that wouldn't save me. When they were strong enough, he said, they'd finish us. He meant it, believe me. He's a general now, and commands a Bison division. Funnily enough, he used exactly the terms that were used again just after Hungary had been crushed. 'We'll bury you,' he said. 'Give us time, we'll bury you:' Just that, no reason given, nothing else.

"Then I saw it spread from Russia. To the Balkans, to Eastern Europe, to China. Troops taken prisoner in Korea forced to stand naked on the ice of a frozen river while water was poured over their feet until they were part of the ice of the river. Until they were prepared to say anything, sign anything, to preserve their sanity. Some of them didn't give in. They lost their feet. Sometimes they lost their minds, sometimes their lives. My nephew was one of the lucky ones. He just lost his life.

"I didn't see what happened in Hungary, but some of my friends did. Remember the wild excitement of the first few days? A torch had been lit, we said. The human spirit is unconquerable after all, we said. The crash as Stalin's statue fell was supposed to be the signal for the re-birth of freedom. Instead, it heralded the entry of the Red Army.

"The armour moved in and slowly crushed the life out of Budapest. Tank crews fired high explosive at crowds of helpless women and children. Some of the Russian troops sickened of their task, and refused to carry on. So the Kremlin fell back on their old standby. In went the Mongolians, and they behaved with their customary savagery. The revolt was smashed.

"The Russians marked the fact we were prepared to sacrifice a nation rather than risk a war. They marked the fact we preferred to preach sermons to the British and French because they'd seen the grip the Reds were getting on

Egypt, and had done something about it. Their I.C.B.M. was coming along fast. Our reluctance to act gave them fresh proof they'd be able to fight a war exactly when and where they chose. They went to work. It was that Christmas of fifty-six I decided they had to be smashed.

"You know what's happened since. Their satellites. Their I.C.B.M. sites almost ready. Their phoney ending of H-tests You're damn right they could afford to end them. In the six weeks before they made the announcement they'd tested enough bombs to keep them going for at least three years. You've seen the figures, you know that's true. And the way they planned things, by the time that three years was up they wouldn't need the bombs any more. They'd have blotted out all opposition."

Quinten paused, picked up his pencil, and began doodling on his notepad again. "That's why I acted, Paul," he went on, his voice quieter and lower pitched than it had been a few seconds before. "Because it was not only expedient, it was right. Because it wasn't wanton aggression, but sheer self-defence. Do you understand?"

Howard stood up. He walked over to the window, and gazed out at the darkness which had flowed over the base when the airfield lighting was turned off. "I think I do," he said levelly. "I think I understand, General, and I'm beginning to think . . ."

He broke off abruptly as in the distance a dozen red flames and two white lines of tracer blazed suddenly in the darkness. Almost at once the thuds of the explosions were heard, and then heavier, louder explosions as a couple of Skysweepers from one of the concrete flak towers joined in. He swung round. "General, we're being attacked."

Quinten looked at the wall clock. Eight minutes after eleven. It was too soon. He wondered how they'd managed to mount an attack so quickly. "I expected it," he murmured, "but not this fast. All right, so we'll hold them off as long as we can. There's no sweat."

Howard looked at him. Quinten was unruffled, not in the least perturbed by the attack. A moment ago, Howard had found Quinten's reasoning valid. He had almost spoken right out in favour of the general's action. But this was something else. Out there Americans were killing Americans. That couldn't be justified ever. He felt a sudden surge of anger at whoever had ordered the attack. And a cold, bitter hatred of Quinten, who was prepared to let his own men die.

He forced himself to speak soberly and quietly. That way Quinten might listen to him. "General, those are our own people out there attacking, and our own people defending. Your plan's safe now. For God's sake stop this unnecessary killing." There was a continual background of noise as he spoke. Out on the wide expanses of the base lines of tracer were appearing in thirty or forty different places.

Quinten sighed. "I don't like it, Paul, any more than you do, but it's necessary. There's still an hour before the eight forty-third bomb. If whoever's attacking can walk right in they might be able to locate Bailey or Hudson in time to get the code group from them. I can't risk that." The telephone on his desk rang. He picked it up. "Sure," he said; "I know what uniforms they're wearing, they're trying to take the base aren't they? . . . All right then, throw in everything we've got . . . Sure, do that" He replaced the phone.

Howard moved slowly over to the desk. Quinten placed his right hand near the automatic, but did not pick it up. "Give orders to stop it, General," Howard said quietly. "There are men dying out there, men who trusted you and believed in you. Don't do this to them."

Quinten shook his head. "They're unlucky, Paul, but they're honoured too. They're dying to save our world. They're dying for peace on earth."

Howard turned away from the desk and went back to the window. Out on the base the fire fight was noisier, more vivid. Both sides were fully committed now. Hot lines of shells stabbed through the air, clawing at their targets, exploding in vicious red flashes as they hit. Howard felt empty and cold. He knew it was no use arguing further. Quinten's resolve was inflexible.

Quinten lit a cigarette. His mental anguish was greater than Howard could suspect. He loved the base, and he loved the men under his command. Each explosion, each rattling burst of automatic fire, stabbed painfully into his mind. Peace on earth, he thought. That's what they're dying for. It's worth it; it has to be. On earth peace, goodwill to all men. A few will suffer, but millions will live. He picked up his pencil. He knew what he was doing was right.

"ALABAMA ANGEL"

11.10 G.M.T.
Moscow: 2.10 p.m.
Washington: 6.10 a.m.

ALABAMA ANGEL reeled under the force of the explosion, her port wing flipping up almost to the vertical as the blast bucked it. The huge aircraft shuddered, shaking with a vibration heavier than any Clint Brown had ever experienced. The cabin was filling with acrid smoke as he brought the plane level, trimmed it for rapid descent, and shouted to Federov for air brakes and reduced revs.

The bomber tilted forward, shuddered again for a few seconds as the air brakes bit into the thin air and disrupted the airflow to slow the plane during rapid descent. Within seconds Brown saw that the inboard portside engine pod had received a lot of the blast. The counters for numbers three and four engines were showing rapidly falling revs, and the fire warning lights were glowing red in the little ports above each counter.

"Shutting down three and four," Federov said calmly. "Fire system operated on three and four."

"Kay." Brown watched the two counters as they wound down to zero. Five seconds later the two red lights winked out. "Seems to be under control, Federov. Everyone on emergency oxygen. Check in as I call you." He listened while the crew members answered in turn. Then he went on, "All right, we're hit. But she's flying. I'm going down to thirty-five. I'll call for damage assessments as soon as we level out. Get working."

He adjusted the trim to give a constant rate of descent of eight thousand feet per minute. The smoke in the cabin did not seem any worse. But the fact it was there at all indicated a failure in the pressure system, probably punctures of the walls of the pressurised section. A glance at the pressure equivalence gauges confirmed the failure. Before the explosion they had indicated an equivalent of a comfortable ten thousand feet. Now they showed a fifteen thousand equivalent, and were climbing rapidly. Brown judged they would reach thirty-five about the same time the bomber got down to that level.

He felt momentarily grateful they had survived the first hazard. The breaks in the pressure walls hadn't been serious enough for explosive decompression to occur. A lucky break there. Explosive decompression at a height of twelve miles, with the cabin pressurised to maintain an apparent height of only two, would have ripped the plane apart. They would all have died instantly. The feeling of gratitude lasted perhaps a tenth of a second. Then it was pushed into the background by the imminent presence of other dangers.

The altimeter needles wound down past forty-five thousand. Whatever happened now, they could breathe. About another minute to go to thirty-five. He glanced quickly round his instruments. Except for the two still needles of the dead engines they appeared normal. He began to feel a small degree of optimism. If the damage was just to the pressure walls and two engines, that wasn't too bad. They could fly a long way on six engines. To the target certainly. And back to the States afterwards? Well, maybe not at thirty thousand feet, but for the moment that wasn't important.

Lieutenant Owens on radar said, "Captain, I've tracked two more missiles. They broke away like the first four."

"Yeah," Brown said. "Keep watching, Bill." He saw the altimeter needle flick down past forty thousand, then grasped the significance of Owens' report. "So your radar's still working? And the brain?"

"Good as new, Captain."

"Fine." Brown pushed another two factors into their slots in the framework plan he was constructing. He thought quickly of the missile which had hit them. The prime fact was the electronic brain had worked. He started from that. He coupled with it the way they had come under fire long before he'd thought they would, way out further to sea than the Intelligence boys had estimated. Also, that Owens was picking up the missiles at a range of only sixty miles, on radar which had an easy pick-up range of a hundred, while they were still about a hundred and fifty miles from the coast.

It added up to the missiles coming from a ship. Maybe the

Russians had stationed a screen of picket ships to extend the range of their coastal defences? Brown didn't think so. The routine reconnaissance missions would have reported them, the same way the Russian reconnaissances had no doubt fixed every Texas Tower and every picket ship in NORAD's organisation.

His mind worked fast on the various possibilities. Now the pay-off was being made for the hours of compulsory study he had put in at SAC intelligence rooms, assimilating the carefully gleaned information about the enemy's weapons; actual, future, and potential. His mind selected, from the mass of information it had stored, a few items which helped to give shape to the problem, and assist in its solution.

Thus. Four cruisers of the Zherdlov class had been converted to anti-aircraft missile ships. The Russians were thought to have in hand a missile which combined infra-red with radar homing. But the date for that missile's operational debut was still a year away. Two of the cruisers converted were based on Archangel. One of them was actively operational, the other carried experimental missiles. Finally, the Russians had been known to use icebreakers to cut a channel to a spot in the middle of a frozen sea, slip a big ship through the channel, and leave it as an artificial island until they decided to cut it out of the thick ice which would reform around it.

It took less than thirty seconds for Brown to decide about the missile which had hit them. Obviously, it had had only a small, high-explosive warhead. An operational missile would have used a nuclear head. Only one had been fired, against six radar-guided missiles. There could be little doubt it was an experimental infra-red missile—the way it had circled and homed in on the radiations from the engines helped establish that—and had been fired from a ship temporarily marooned in the ice-locked Barents Sea for trials.

The altimeter was showing thirty-six thousand as he said to Federov, "Brakes in. Get me the revs for maximum speed at this altitude." He watched the needle approach the thirty-five thousand and trimmed the aircraft into level flight.

"Captain, you know the fuel consumption if we use maximum speed this height?" Federov's voice was anxious.

"I know it. But with the drop in height and two engines out we're going to need every mile not to miss out too badly on our bomb time. Any ideas about the wind at this level, Stan?"

Lieutenant Stan Andersen glanced briefly at the sector graphs of the vertical air mass structure. "Shouldn't hurt us," he said briefly. "May help. There wasn't much going our way at sixty."

"O.K., I'll take damage reports. Normal crew rotation." He listened to the reports from the crew, carefully weighing each report, asking questions to clear any point he wanted checked.

The defence system was in good shape. The brain was working, and so was the search radar. Goldsmith's two hornets were still ready to go, with all their circuits in order. The remaining eight weapons seemed to be all right.

Mellows reported the radio working satisfactorily. Lieutenant Engelbach was a little unhappy about his target radar. The bombsight mechanisms seemed unaffected, but the radar-scope wasn't functioning well. He said he'd be able to tell better when they had crossed in over land.

Andersen was satisfied with his navigation equipment, and Federov confirmed the plane was flying fine except for the two dead engines. "They know how to build these things at Boeing," he said. "Take a lot more than that to kill a fifty-two."

"Yeah," Brown said. "Sure, a lot more." He thought for a long moment about his girl at Seattle. He remembered the way she would say, "Clint honey, I'll never be jealous of the airplane, or the eight forty-third, or any other old wing they assign you to. I grew up with airplanes here. I guess I can live with them when we're married."

When we're married. How did Seattle look now? High shattered buildings poking a few ferro-concrete fingers at a sky loaded with strontium dust? Tarmac of roads, stone and wood of houses, bone and sinew of human flesh, fused into a smooth, dead amalgam? Glowing black hair and tall graceful body, brain and voice and generous, loving heart, charred into black nothing? Brown said tightly, "Garcia?"

"They're O.K., Captain," Garcia said quietly.

"All right. Thanks, Garcia." Brown glanced round the instruments again, waiting for the important words from Andersen and Federov. A minute went by while he tried not to think about Seattle. For all but five seconds of the minute he failed.

Andersen came in first. "We can't make it before ten after twelve. Even with the boost in speed the loss of height has cut us down. It would be more, but the wind seems pretty good at this level."

"O.K., Stan." Brown fitted the last but one factor into his framework. Now he was only waiting on Federov. He waited another half minute before he got the news he had been fearing, about as he expected it from his own rough calculations.

"Two thousand eight hundred from target," Federov said. "I've made allowance we drop speed once we leave the target. Add eight hundred from A point to target, still leaves us way over a thousand under minimum."

Over a thousand under minimum. That ruled out return to any base south of the fiftieth parallel. And the bases north of it would probably be out already. Well, if it came to the worst, they could always drop altitude and hit the silk once they got back over land. The airplane wouldn't matter then, it would have done its job. He looked at his count-down clock. Fifty-one to run. He found it difficult to work back from that, to translate the minutes to target into actual time. He could quite easily have glanced at his watch. But it simply did not occur to him. He said, "Stan, time check. And how many minutes before we cross in?"

Stan Andersen broke off his work, checked his wristwatch against the small chronometer located in the bottom right hand corner of the ground position indicator. "Coming up to 11.15. Ten seconds . . . Five . . . Now. Set the count-down to fifty-five. And we cross in at 11.24. Couple of minutes later than I estimated. There'll be a small change of course shortly but not very much. Two or three degrees."

"Right, Stan. O.K., men, this is how it goes. We're still capable of hitting our primary target, maybe the secondary too, but certainly the primary. That's got to be hit. Here's how I see it.

"I'm pretty goddam sure we were hit by an experimental missile, and I don't figure on running up against any more like that. I'm confident we can divert their ordinary missiles, and we know Goldsmith's little stingers can blot out the fighters they'll send up. Everything else is working fine, so we'll hit our primary.

"All right, that looks good, so what are the snags? First, we got hit and we got holed in the pressure cabin. We're twenty-five thousand under our best operating altitude, but that's the way it has to be. That won't stop us geting to the primary.

"We'll get there, but—an' I'm not going to mince words about this—we may not make a useable base afterwards. You know what a drop in altitude does to the fuel consumption of a jet engine. If we can't make a base, I'm planning on dropping height and letting everyone bale out once we get over friendly land.

"That's the aeronautical side, now here's the tactical. There's no reason they can hit us any better at this height than at sixty thousand. Only reason we flew up there was to stretch fuel. Tactically, we're as safe down here. Maybe safer, because they won't expect us in at this altitude."

Brown paused, then went on slowly, "So I'm going right on in to the primary. We could turn back now, and with good reason, but I'm not going to. Our target is the I.C.B.M. site at Kotlass. We don't hit it, we'll maybe help to kill an awful lot of our own people. So we're going on."

Lieutenant Bill Owens broke in on him. Urgently. "Captain, I have two blips, must be fighters. They're well apart, coming head on. Speed high, about Mach Two. Range fifty."

"Roger," Brown said. "Your hornets ready to go, Goldsmith?"

"Ready, Captain." Goldsmith checked over his instruments for the twentieth time. Everything functioning right. He flicked down the fire switches of one and six to the on position. It only needed a stab of the button now.

"They're in to twenty five," Owens said. "Moving further apart. Guess they must be under close control, going to pass and come in from port and starboard together."

"Right," Brown said.

"Call them at ten." Goldsmith's voice was lifting, eager.

"Twelve now, going further out. You have them, Herman?"

"Sure," Goldsmith said happily. "I have them." He watched the two bright dots on his fire control scope. They were following the classic attack pattern of the supersonic missile-carrying fighter. Break off from ahead of target, start to turn hard in when you got abeam, come in with six hundred miles of overtake speed, launch your rockets, get out fast.

Goldsmith watched them almost lovingly as they turned in, one from port, one from starboard. That tactic wouldn't confuse the missiles. They had a preference system built into them which would incline them towards targets on their own side of the bomber. The fighters were at six miles now. Goldsmith put his two thumbs on the firing buttons. Five and a half miles. Five. He said, "Firing," and pressed the two buttons.

Electricity raced along the circuit wires which connected the missiles with the bomber. From the firing ports of each motor twelve white flames licked hungrily back into the air stream. The slim rockets slid neatly out of their embracing tubes, and roared away on their destructive task.

Goldsmith peered closely at his scope. He saw the two small blobs of light march across the screen towards the bigger blobs, hesitate for a moment, then dart firmly in to mingle with them.

Behind *Alabama Angel* two red balls of fire expanded slowly in the cold wastes of the air. Two rockets went into the self immolation which was their destined end. With them they took two Soviet all-weather fighters. The pilots of the fighters, Goldsmith thought, as he watched the sudden violent reaction on his scope, would never have known what hit them. He said, "Fighters destroyed. I'll line up the next two."

Goldsmith selected two and seven on the row of switches half way down his panel. The red lights glowed steadily beneath each of them. He waited the twenty seconds necessary to prime and place the missiles in firing positions. The red lights continued to glow. He switched in to emergency circuits. No effect. He cancelled the selection of two and seven, tried three and eight. Four and nine. Five and ten. The red lights glowed.

He spent another minute playing with the switches, cutting in circuits and taking them out, trying all the four emergency procedures. Then he said, quietly but definitely, "Captain, there's a foul up with the hornets. I figure it as damage to the positioning arms. Whatever it is, they're out."

Goldsmith finished speaking. Brown was considering what that would imply, when Lieutenant Owens said, "Captain, another fighter coming in. Fast, like the other two. Forty miles ahead."

THE PENTAGON

11.15 G.M.T.
Moscow: 2.15 p.m.
Washington: 6.15 a.m.

THE RUSSIAN AMBASSADOR to the United States, M. Zorubin, had only been accredited in Washington a few months longer than the President had held office. So far he had created a good impression. He was a tall, florid, jovial seeming man, with an excellent command of English which he spoke with a slight British accent—the results of an eight year spell of duty in London.

He was a man of striking personality, and he contrived to put into the simplest statements a warmth and sincerity which convinced the listener that here was a man who meant what he said. As a home-grown, small town politician, he would have been strong on kissing babies and firm man-to-man handshakes. As a diplomat holding one of the most important appointments in the world, he confined his kissing to the fingers of senators' wives, who found his gallantry and his witty conversation full of charm.

The President liked Zorubin personally, but he did not altogether trust him. Wit and elegance have never distinguished the State Department, where the austere, puritanical tradition seems to continue through the years. The President and the Secretary of State preferred diplomats to be serious, sober men. Also, they were not sure just how much Zorubin counted for among the inner circles at the Kremlin. They suspected he was a person of no importance, who had been posted to Washington simply as a figurehead, to convince the American public that a man so pleasant and so cultured must surely represent a peace loving and reasonable government.

It so happened they were wrong. Zorubin stood close to the hub of power in the Kremlin. He had realised early in his political life that alliances were dangerous, and enmities even more so. He had carefully avoided contracting any alliances or even any close friendships except one. His gay insouciance, and his apparent lack of interest in internal politics, had ensured he made no enemies.

Thus he was able to survive the murderous intrigues of Stalin's early years, the massive purges that three times convulsed Russia while Stalin was at the height of his power, and even the bloody, internecine fighting which immediately followed Stalin's death. Finally, the Marshal had attained supreme power, gathering the reins of government into his pudgy but efficient hands. Zorubin had survived to triumph, for it was with the Marshal he had formed his only close friendship. And, since he had never taken any part in internal politics, had in fact only spent about two years of the previous twenty in Russia, it was a friendship which would last. The Marshal had no cause whatever to fear him, and so he was safe. As a token of that friendship he had been given the Washington appointment, and his dispatches were highly valued.

The valuation placed on his reports was not entirely due to friendship. Beneath Zorubin's charm and elegance was hidden a first class brain, icy cold, detached, and when necessary, ruthless. Since his arrival in Washington his evaluations and predictions of United States Policy had proved uncannily accurate. The Marshal gave great weight to his judgments.

Now, in the fifteen minutes he had been in the War Room, Zorubin was as near frightened as he had been for years. The President had explained fully what had happened. He had convinced Zorubin of his good faith, that he was making every effort to recall the bombers. The difficulty was, of course, that the bombers apparently could not be recalled. And Zorubin was worried. There were certain things he knew, certain actions which might be taken. Later, if it became necessary to prod the President into some unpleasant action, he might find it necessary to inform him of them. For the moment, however, the President seemed to be doing all he could. Zorubin decided to wait a while.

The President, the Secretary of State, and the Russian Ambassador, were closeted in a small cube-shaped room within the War Room itself. Army Signals had provided two microphones and two speakers. These were linked to a radio net flung across an ocean and a continent to the Kremlin. The Joint Chiefs, with General Franklin in attendance as commander of SAC, sat on the opposite side of the table.

Zorubin had arrived just as the President spoke to the Marshal for the first time. The exchanges had been polite, but formal. Zorubin, listening keenly, had been unable to detect any particular emotion in the Marshal's voice.

But he knew his friend too well to be deceived by that.

He had acted as interpreter for the President. At his suggestion the American Ambassador in Moscow had been summoned to the Kremlin to interpret for the Marshal. It had been generally agreed that the matters under discussion were too important for any but the highest placed to hear them.

The President had explained briefly what had happened He outlined the measures he had taken, and was taking, to bring the bombers back. He stressed that the United States did not by any means seek a war with Soviet Russia, and to show his good faith he had invited the Soviet Ambassador to the Pentagon so that he could witness exactly what efforts were being made to stop the attack.

"You say only thirty-two of your bombers are involved. Where are the rest of them?" the Marshal asked.

"I have grounded them," the President replied quickly. He thought there was no possibility that any of the SAC wings which were airborne could be seen on Russia radar.

"My staff report at least another two hundred in the air," the Marshal snapped.

Zorubin smiled briefly. The Americans had no monopoly of early warning systems. Keppler grinned at Steele, whose expression remained imperturbable. "They are in the air, yes," the President said. "But they are on their way back. They are not heading towards Russia."

"Well, we will see." The reply was grudging.

"Marshal, I have already conveyed my sincere regrets that this thing has happened. May I suggest we now consider only how we can best ensure that the bombers do not reach their targets. We will continue to do everything we can to recall them by radio. But I have also arranged for my staff to prepare a complete list of the bombers' targets and approach routes, heights, and speeds. They will pass these on to your staff, together with details of the defensive weapons carried by the planes." The President paused, and his voice faltered slightly. It is never a pleasant thing to be forced to sacrifice your own troops. "You will thus be able to make dispositions to intercept and destroy the bombers before they reach their targets. We feel we cannot ask you to wait until we know whether we can recall the bombers by radio, so we accept the need for you to destroy the bombers as quickly as is possible. The information we will give you should help you to do this."

"We will see." Again the grudging reply. "How soon can you pass the information?"

"Immediately you are ready for it."

"We are ready now. My staff tell me they are in contact with yours. Is there anything more?"

"Yes," the President said slowly. "There is. We have admitted we were at fault. But I think we have shown we are prepared to do everything in our power to put right that fault. Now I must ask for proof of good faith on your part. I would consider that ordering your long range bombers to remain on the ground would be sufficient proof."

Zorubin looked momentarily startled. It seemed he was about to protest the President's request. But the tone in which the words had been spoken precluded any argument. Zorubin shrugged, and waited for the reply. When it came, he was surprised. There was none of the indignation he had expected. Instead, the Marshal said merely, "We will see. Your Ambassador has now arrived. I am having him brought in with me." And there, for the moment, the matter rested.

The President felt very tired. Already, in his few weeks at the White House, he had realised he would never again be able to live a life free from worry and responsibility of the heaviest, most killing kind. He knew now why previous Presidents had aged so quickly, and been so subject to failures of health. The grotesque thought passed through his mind of an advertising campaign of the before and after photograph type, to dissuade ambitious politicians who saw in the Presidency only a chance for self glorification. He offered Zorubin a cigarette, and lit it for him, as the small bulb in the pedestal of Keppler's phone winked on and off.

The burly general took the phone in a big fist. "Keppler here," he growled, and then listened in silence to the message. Fifteen seconds went by before he said, "Wait," and covered the mouthpiece with the palm of his left hand.

"Mr. President, they've run into trouble at Sonora. They've taken a lot of casualties, and the battalion commander reports he's pinned down. He has to put down smoke to give him a chance of breaking through without getting his troops murdered. It's going to take time to do."

The President glanced at the wall clock. It showed eleven twenty-one. Again, he had to make an unpleasant decision. With less than forty minutes left there was no time to spare. "How long will it take?"

Keppler shrugged. "It depends on the state of the wind. Five minutes, possibly ten. He's already started to put it down."

"Order him to advance immediately," the President said. "He is to regard his troops as expendable. I want them in control as fast as possible."

Keppler nodded, spoke briefly into the phone. His eyes were sad. The ranger units were his personal charges. It is hard to assist at the execution of one of your children.

Zorubin was pleased. The President meant business, clearly enough. He began to feel a faint hope that triumph might yet be plucked from disaster. "In Russia also, we would not allow military operations to be influenced by sentiment," he said approvingly.

"In Russia you wouldn't know what the damn word means," Keppler snarled, his face purple.

"General!" The President's voice cracked like a whip. "You will control yourself, if you please."

Keppler glowered at the table. He muttered something which might have passed as an apology. Strangely enough it was General Franklin who came to his aid.

"The general's remark was understandable," Franklin said coldly. "He feels the same way about his troops as I do about my crews. And His Excellency forgets we are all well informed about Russia not allowing military operations to be influenced by sentiment. As in Hungary, no doubt."

"Now that will do," the President said flatly. "Franklin, however justified you may consider your remarks, they were uncalled for. We are here to resolve a crisis, not to continue . . ." The President halted abruptly. He realsied he had been about-to put in a reference to the futile bickering which had made nonsense of international conferences in the past decade. He smiled suddenly, as the absurdity of the situation gripped him. "Franklin, you'll apologise to His Excellency," he ended.

"That will not be necessary," Zorubin said quickly. "General Franklin, like General Keppler, is a soldier. He says what he means, from the heart. Not like we diplomats, Mr. President. Please, I am the guest here, and I have the privileges of a guest. I insist, no apology is necessary." His voice was convincing and sincere.

Franklin smiled. "It is kind of His Excellency," he said formally. "But he'll find *he* has to apologise if he goes on calling me a soldier. I don't think General Keppler would agree at all with that description."

"Well," Keppler said, "I don't know. After all, you

started in the Army." His tone was warm and friendly. He was pleased by the way Franklin had risked the anger of the President to stand by him.

An orderly was escorted into the room by a white helmeted M.P. Mugs of steaming coffee were served to the men round the table. The orderly and the M.P. withdrew. The hands of the wall clock moved on to eleven twenty-four.

Outside, in the War Room proper, the staffs were at work. The target routes of every individual bomber had been faithfully relayed to the Russians. The heights and speeds which the bombers would be flying had been passed on, together with the information about the 52K's defence system. Signals had done a first class job in providing channels of communication, and their counterparts in Moscow had surprised everyone by the speed and efficiency with which they had handled the hook-up at their end.

Soon questions began to come back, to supplement the information already supplied, and clarify points of difficulty. Most commonly these questions were easily dealt with after a mistake in translation had been rectified. Nine tenths of the queries raised were due to translation errors. The other tenth was not.

When a dozen or more staff officers are asking questions simultaneously without any central control of their questions, the intelligence officers can soon distinguish and isolate any recurrent pattern of thought, and interpret its significance. Now, as the questions came in, an Air Force colonel and his two assistants subjected them to scrutiny. They detected a pattern, isolated it, considered the constant stream of new questions in the light of that pattern. Very soon, they had arrived at a definite conclusion. The report of the first contact between the Russian defences and an 843rd bomber confirmed that conclusion.

General Steele, the Air Force Chief of Staff, picked up

his telephone in response to the insistent winking of the call light. "All right," he said, "bring it on in."

A few moments later the Air Force colonel who had evaluated the Russian questions came into the room. He whispered to Steele, pointing out things on the clipboard he was carrying. "O.K., leave it with me," Steele said finally. The colonel left the room.

Steele stood up. "Mr. President, the intelligence boys have come to certain conclusions There is also a report of contact between the Russian defences and one of our bombers."

"Well, let's hear it." The President's voice was eager.

"First, a bomber flying south towards Kolguev Island has been hit. They don't say whether it was destroyed. Intelligence thinks it was certainly the result of a weapon fired from a guided missiles trial ship in the Barents Sea. No other contact with our attacking forces has been reported.

"Intelligence feels this weapon was one which embodied some form of guidance system other than purely electronic. From the questions the Russians have been asking they feel sure that most of the Russian missiles, if not all, will be susceptible to interference by the electronic brains carried in the bombers. We already know, of course, that there is little a fighter can do to evade the infra-red guidance missiles carried by the bombers." Steele sat down.

"Then it appears likely they will be able to penetrate to their targets, even with the information we have supplied?"

"It appears so," Steele said.

"It is so." Zorubin spoke flatly and definitely.

"You mean," the President asked, "that your defences do not include ground to air missiles of a type other than radar guided?"

"To the best of my knowledge, no." Zorubin looked round the table. "I am not a military expert, but naturally I know roughly where we stand. I have heard that missiles using other types of guidance were put in hand last year when we happened to hear about the brain you were building into your bombers. I would not think they were ready yet."

Happened to hear. Well, that was one way of putting it, the President thought. "So it looks like a lot depends on Sonora," he said aloud.

"Everything, Mr. President. Believe me, literally everything in the world."

The men round the table looked surprised, and then shocked. Because it was Zorubin who had spoken, or rather cried out, those words. And all of them realised at once that Zorubin was mortally afraid.

" ALABAMA ANGEL "

11.20 G.M.T.
Moscow: 2.20 p.m.
Washington: 6.20 a.m.

CLINT BROWN asked calmly, "Any hope of the hornets coming unstuck, Herman?"

"I just don't know, Captain." Goldsmith spoke fast and nervously. "Guess I'd better go take a look in back."

"O.K. What range is the hostile now?"

"Thirty," Lieutenant Owens said. "Closing about a mile every two seconds."

Brown figured quickly. A minute to come level. Half a minute extra as the fighter turned away, another minute as it turned and caught up. Add a half minute for pilot re-action being slowed after turning hard at those speeds. About three minutes to attack. He had to go down soon. "O.K., Herman," he said, "go on back. I'll give you thirty seconds, then I'm starting down. Plug in back there and let me know."

"Roger." Goldsmith moved quickly to the armoured bulk-head separating the pressure cabin from the main fuselage. He took with him a mobile oxygen kit and a spare intercom set.

Brown heard Owens call the fighter at twenty-five miles. He said, "Stand by for maximum rate descent. All set, Fed-erov?"

"All set, Captain. I'll give you six thousand revs on the descent. You can pull them back another thousand if you need to."

"All right." Brown sat watching the seconds tick away on his watch. Maximum descent was fourteen thousand feet per minute. If Goldsmith couldn't untangle the hornets, it was the only answer. At thirty-five thousand *Alabama Angel* was a sitting duck. At ground level the fighter's radar would be confused by ground returns which would blot out the air-craft blip. To fly really low was full of hazards. Bad visibility, uncertain navigation, high ground on the route. But it was the only chance.

As if reading his thoughts, Andersen piped up. "We'll cross in just after getting down on the deck. There's a thin layer of cloud at eighteen thousand, but there shouldn't be much under that. Visibility should be good this time of year. There won't be a lot of light, but there's no high ground to worry about for the first ten minutes."

"Thanks, Stan." Brown waited for Owens to call the ten miles. He decided five seconds after that he'd begin to go down. He'd have to watch his Mach number very carefully.

Normally, the 52 was well behaved right up to point nine
six of the speed of sound. But the blast damage might have
roughened up the airflow. He'd have to be alert for the first
hint of vibration which would indicate compressibility
troubles.

"Ten miles," Owens said. "Moving away to starboard."

"Roger." Brown's hand went to the trim control. He
counted off the seconds. With two left he said, "Going down,"
and thumbed the trim control forward. "Remember we
aren't pressurised. Keep swallowing. I can't go back up for
anyone with ear trouble."

The descent indicator moved round until it showed a rate
of fourteen thousand feet per minute. Brown trimmed the
bomber into the right position to maintain that rate of
descent. He watched the Machmeter carefully as it moved up
from point nine. Almost immediately he felt the judder. The
Machmeter was indicating only point nine three. He said,
"Cut back on revs, Federov."

"Cutting."

Lieutenant Goldsmith reported in from the rear fuselage.
"Captain, the hornets are snarled but good. A piece of
metal from that missile got the main feed servo. Nothing I
can do about it, so I'm coming back up."

Brown acknowledged the message, and concentrated on
his speed and rate of descent. He thought maybe the air
brakes had been hit too. Something was definitely wrong.
Working closely with Federov he cut back the revs to the
danger point. They could not bring them down any lower
without risking a flame-out. But the speed still built up too
fast. Gradually, Brown trimmed back until at a descent rate
of ten thousand per minute the plane was holding a steady
point nine one. There was little vibration. It was a comparatively slow rate of descent, but it would have to do. Anything faster meant shaking the bomber to pieces.

"Hostile at twelve miles, four o'clock," Owens said. "Turning in."

Brown frowned, glanced at the altimeter. Still at twenty-seven thousand. He hoped the Russian pilot wouldn't turn too tight, and wasn't too expert at recovering and straightening out on the attack run.

"Thirteen miles, five o'clock," Owens said. "Straightening out." He paused for a few seconds, watching the scope with a concentration so intense he was oblivious to anything except the menacing brightness of the hostile echo. He saw it move ever more slowly over to six o'clock, with the range going out only slightly. "Six o'clock, now, fourteen miles. Captain, this boy's turning real fast."

"Yeah," Brown said. "He straight now?"

"Sure, coming in straight. I'll call him at ten and every mile after."

Brown noted the height. Twenty-three thousand. He quickly calculated the time needed to get the bomber down to ground level against the time the fighter needed to reach firing position. It was a simple problem. The fighter would be closing them at about ten miles a minute. Say he let fly at two miles range. That meant only a little more than seventy seconds before firing point. In seventy seconds the bomber would be down to an altitude of ten thousand feet. It was too high.

Suddenly, Brown was afraid. For the first time in his life he felt the physical impact of naked fear. For the first time he experienced the special refinement of agony which fear can produce in a normally brave man. He recognised it for what it was, rationalised it, and concentrated with all his determination on the job he had in hand. He did not conquer the fear, but he pushed it far enough in the background so he could continue to function efficiently.

"Ten miles," Owen called.

Ten miles. And *Alabama Angel* still at nineteen thousand. There wasn't a chance of getting low enough. Desperately he sought for something he had overlooked, something which would enable him to outguess the electronic devices in the fighter behind him. But he knew there was nothing. The anti-missiles brain could swamp the low powered signals from missiles, impose its own will upon them by sheer force. But the Russians had fighters—a new supersonic series, one of which was probably boring in on them now—equipped with radar too powerful for the brain to deceive.

"Eight miles." Owens' voice was brittle; positive but troubled.

Brown admitted to himself there was nothing he could do to counter the threat except to try and judge the moment when the figher would loose its rockets. With the admission came an immediate release of tension, and a slackening of the tight embrace which fear had locked around him. He heard Owens count the fighter in to seven miles, five, three. He braced himself for quick action.

"Goldsmith," he said urgently. "Shout 'now' at any sign of rocket release."

"Roger."

Brown trimmed the bomber neutral, maintained the downward path by pressure on the controls. There was just one chance. The Russian pilot's automatic predictor sight would have computed the downward progress of the airplane. It would aim his rockets at a point where the bomber should be if it continued downwards. "Give me full power when I start nosing up, Federov," he said.

"Now," Goldsmith screamed down the intercom.

Brown heaved back on the stick, felt the fast build up of centrifugal force press him heavily down in his seat. The plane flattened out of the descent, lifted its nose reluctantly towards the sky, and began to climb. He counted the seconds as the salvo of rockets accelerated towards them, found his brain was working so fast he had time to assess the chances of the rockets carrying nuclear warhead. He put them pretty low.

The main salvo of rockets passed harmlessly beneath the bomber, too far away for the proximity fuses to fire them. Three, flying higher than the rest, detonated as they passed underneath. They did not cause any damage. A fourth, possibly through some defect in its stabilisers, came in higher and slower than the others. It exploded ten yards off the starboard side of the rear end of the pressure cabin, the twenty kilo charge erupting its steel case into a hundred lethal pieces.

The blast gouged out whole sections of the fuselage and starboard wing. Between twenty and thirty jagged lumps of steel tore through the cabin. Mellows, Goldsmith, and Minter died at once, their bodies ripped open by the furious metal. Andersen was untouched, but Garcia was hit in the leg. Federov received only a slight flesh wound. Engelbach and Owens were not hit, but a fragment wrecked Owens' main radar.

Brown felt a slamming impact in his back, which knocked him forward to slump unconscious against the controls. And *Alabama Angel*, responsive to the forward movement of the stick, pushed her nose down again, and began the long, sickening slide into the hostile darkness beneath.

It was Federov who recovered first from the shock of the explosion. He stumbled forward to the pilot's seat, heaved Brown out, and lowered him gently to the floor. Freed of Brown's weight on the controls, the nose of the bomber began slowly to lift towards the horizontal, in obedience to the urge of the trimmers. Federov, panting with the effort of moving Brown, climbed into the seat. He was vaguely conscious of Andersen bending over the unconscious pilot.

Federov knew he had to act fast. The fighter might be circling for another strike. Or other fighters might be heading in on the target. Federov was no pilot, but like all SAC engineers he had been given a hundred or so hours dual. He could look after the plane in the air if he was not called on to land it, or to perform really tight combat flying. And he knew the safest place was near the ground. O.K., that's where he'd head for. He eased the stick forward, trimming the aircraft into a nose down position at the same time. Again *Alabama Angel* tilted down into the darkness.

Next, Federov assessed the damage. Amazingly, all six engines were still functioning normally. He felt the onset of compressibility vibration, and hastily cut back the revs of the engines. The juddering stopped. He made a quick and thorough inspection of the instruments. All the flying instruments were all right. Fuel feeds seemed to be normal.

Temperatures and pressures were about right. Federov sighed with relief. The plane was still flying and still flyable. He settled to the task of holding her steadily on course as she lost height. It did not occur to him even to consider turning back.

Andersen, bending over Brown, saw his eyes suddenly blink open. Brown moved his head slowly to one side, looking up past Andersen's face to where Federov sat in the pilot's seat. His lips moved soundlessly, the words lost without trace in the roaring noise of the cabin. Then he began to ease himself up. Andersen moved a hand in protest, urging him to stay down. Brown brushed it impatiently away, and motioned Andersen to help him. Andersen hauled him him slowly upright, and Brown tapped Federov to indicate he wanted to resume the seat. It was only as he climbed into the seat that Andersen saw the dark, spreading stains on his torn clothing half way up the right side of his back.

Brown sank into his seat. He was not yet feeling any pain

beyond a dull ache. But he knew he was hit hard. He felt as though someone had broken off a spear point in his back. It did not hurt, but he was conscious of a bulk which had intruded itself into his body where it had no place to be. He fumbled for the intercom set which had torn away when Federov removed him a few moments before, and checked it was properly connected. Then he said, "Stan, where are we?"

"We've crossed in," Andersen said quickly. "Hold this course a while, unless . . ." he let the sentence tail off.

Brown made no reply. He glanced at the altimeter, then flicked on his radio altimeter. It was working. He remembered that the aerials were out on the port wing tip. Mercifully, they'd not been damaged by the explosion. It made all the difference. Now he could hold an accurate height above ground. Three thousand feet now, and he found he could see quite well. Andersen had been wrong about the cloud. There were a few patches up above, but the stars shone through with the clean, hard brightness of the northern latitudes. The snow on the ground helped too, though it was likely to be deceptive when judging distances.

He said, "Unless nothing, Stan. For the moment we go on. I don't have to tell you how important it is we get through. Right now, we might be the only people standing between Russia and the destruction of the States. We have to go on, and we have to take that base out. It's our duty, and by God we're going to do it."

"Sure," Andersen said. "Sure, Clint. Is there enough light to fly low. Real low, I mean?"

"There's enough," Brown said shortly. His face twisted in pain as a sudden hot shaft of agony stabbed into his back. Here we go, he thought grimly. It was not the first time he had been wounded. When he was only sixteen his brother had accidentally punched a twenty-two slug through his leg while they were out hunting. The first few minutes had been fine. Just a kind of numbness. He had even laughed and joked. The next six hours, before they finally got back to medical aid, had been unadulterated hell.

He said quickly, before the next shaft of pain should hit, "Let's round up on the damage and the casualties. See what's working. I'm going to run in to the target at deck level. Ten miles away, I'll climb up to bomb, let her go, then turn and come back out on the deck. Flight plan on that, will you Stan?"

"Right away." Andersen's hand reached out for his computer.

"All right then," Brown said. He paused, gasping as the pain hit him again, then went on, "We'll make it, men. Believe me, we'll make it and take that base out. Back home right now, they're relying on us to get through, because we know just how important they consider that particular base. And they *can* rely on us. Because we will."

SONORA, TEXAS

11.25 G.M.T.
Moscow: 2.25 p.m.
Washington: 6.25 a.m.

WHEN THE President had taken the decision to send the Rangers into Sonora, General Keppler had said his men would brush the defence aside without too much trouble. General Franklin had insisted there would be heavy casualties. Both generals had been partly right.

The Rangers had moved fast across terrain unfamiliar to them. Wherever they could, they had bypassed troublesome machine-gun emplacements and flak towers. Where they could not, they had brushed them aside. They had taken casualties in the process.

The men of Dog Company, in particular, advancing southeast towards the administration building, had run into trouble when they were caught on the smooth, naked concrete of the 839th Wing's servicing area by the cross fire of two flak towers, each of which mounted two Skysweepers. There was no cover for them on the huge, flat expanse of concrete. They could not dig in, they could not even rely on the earth absorbing some of the hail of shells which ripped into them. The shells exploded instantly on contact with the concrete, and the air became a singing inferno of metal. Dog Company lost sixty per cent of its effective strength in the first minute, and the survivors hastily withdrew under cover of smoke.

The other companies had better luck, but they also took a constant trickle of casualties, which might at any moment become a flood if they were caught on open concrete as Dog Company had been. An airfield by its very nature is usually flat. Sonora was exceptionally flat, and a great part of the flat ground was coated with concrete in the form of runways, servicing areas, fuelling areas, and readiness pens. There was very little cover, and the flak towers mounted as much firepower altogether as would normally be allocated to a division.

The battalion commander, an officer who had seen action in North Africa and Italy, and later in Korea, assessed the casualties reported to him over the walkie-talkie, and decided he must slow up. The only fast line of advance was across the concrete where Dog Company had perished. But advance on that line was impossible while the two flak towers dominated it. He considered how they could be neutralised.

It was a tough problem. The concrete towers had been designed to stand up to a ten kiloton blast at five hundred yards from zero, the kind of blast a tactical atomic weapon might be expected to deliver. They were vulnerable from above, but with the magnificent field of fire they possessed, no mortar crew could hope to live at a range where they could drop their mortar bombs accurately into the circular gun nest. The only answer was smoke. And enough smoke took time to put down. The battalion commander decided it would just have to take time. He gave the orders.

Howard was watching the battle from the window of Quinten's office. It was perfectly safe to remain there, as Quinten had explained to him. When the main object of an attack is to secure the opposing commander alive, the headquarters of that commander is most certainly not a target. One or two stray bullets had smacked into the wall of the building, but that was all.

Like most infantry battles, the fight at Sonora was quite meaningless to the observer who was not himself an infantryman. By the light of constantly erupting flares, Howard had seen a group of men wither away under the fire of two of the flak towers. He had no real idea of the significance of their withdrawal, or of the strange inactivity which followed it.

He turned as Quinten's telephone rang, and heard Quinten receive information and give fresh orders. The general looked directly at him. "We're taking a lot of casualties, Paul," he said. "They're within five hundred yards of this building now. The Security Officer thinks they're re-grouping." His voice was quiet, and with the suspicion of a tremor in it. It was the voice of a man who is infinitely weary, and infinitely sad.

Howard felt a sudden, strange compassion for Quinten.

It pushed into the background the cold anger which he had been nursing. "Call it off now," he said. "Call it off now, Quint." Without realising it, he used the general's nickname.

Quinten smiled at him momentarily. "You're a good boy, Paul," he said. "You'll go a long way. One day you'll have to make a decision, and it may be a decision you don't want to make. When that time comes, remember what's happening now. Make the decision, no matter what it costs you personally. And once you've made it then stick with it.

"A lot of those men out there, whether they're enlisted men or officers, are my friends. I know them, and their wives, and their families. I've helped them get married, been a godparent to their children, chewed them out when they've tied one on and missed duty. The fact they're dying hurts me personally. I couldn't live with what I've done to them. But I have to see things whole, and see them clearly. I've made my decision and I have to stick with it. Look, I'll go this far with you. There's a lull now, and no-one's getting hurt. It's coming up to eleven thirty-one. Average bomb time for the 843rd is five after twelve. I don't figure they'll be able to locate Bailey or Hudson inside thirty minutes, so I'll authorise a cease-fire at eleven thirty-five. Does that help?"

Howard turned to look out of the window again. There was a grey wall of smoke where he had seen the two flak towers catch a bunch of men on the concrete plain that was the 839th servicing area. Occasionally the crack of single carbine or M.1 shots was heard from different parts of the base. Airmen shooting at shadows most likely. "It helps," he said shortly. "Let's hope it stays quiet until then."

He lit a cigarette, and continued to watch the thick grey smoke as it gently stirred in the almost breezeless air. Three flares shone with a dazzling white incandescence, and slowly sank down towards the ground. When they were only fifty or sixty feet up a skirmish line of soldiers suddenly broke out of the smoke, spaced well apart, all moving in different directions, yet purposefully, as if to a well co-ordinated plan.

Five more flares burst in the air, and two searchlights played on the wall of smoke. The Skysweepers opened up, their rapid, staccato thumping interspersed with the lighter rattle of heavy machine-gun and B.A.R. fire. Howard realised he could no longer see the soldiers who had broken out from the smoke, and at the same moment the two search-lights died out with a crash of recoilless rifle shells, and the flares were shot out by a hail of small arms fire.

More flares went up, and in the few brief moments be-fore they were shot out Howard saw the concrete swarming with soldiers who had emerged from the protecting smoke. Before the Skysweepers had fired more than a few rounds darkness again screened them from the defenders. But in that short while Howard had seen a dozen or more men knocked down by the fire.

He swung round suddenly. "Stop it, goddam it," he shouted. He raved at Quinten, calling him every name he could lay his tongue to. Only the big, steady mouth of the point four five prevented him leaping over the table. He was shaking with rage.

Quinten looked at the clock. Eleven thirty-four. "Calm down, Paul," he said. "I'm stopping it. As of now."

Howard rested a hand on the desk. He felt emotionally ex-hausted, completely used up, as helpless and weak as a kitten. He was only vaguely conscious of the incessant firing of the Skysweepers and the steady yammer of light auto-matics.

Quinten flicked the tab of the address system. "This is the Commanding Officer," he said firmly. "This is General Quin-ten speaking. I order a general cease fire. I repeat, you are to cease fire. Remain in your positions, but do not fire any more. You will receive word of mouth orders to that effect from your officers and noncoms as soon as I can get them out. I repeat, this is the Commanding Officer. Cease fire. This is General Quinten. Cease fire."

The great steel voices of the address speakers boomed Quinten's orders across the base. Most personnel heard them, and remained a discreet distance from those positions which were still firing.

Howard and Quinten heard the fire gradually diminish. It did not stop altogether, but it abated. Quinten broadcast a second message, and after that firing became desultory and confined only to small arms. Each of the flak towers had an address speaker, so the gun crews had heard the message and had obeyed its orders.

"I've got a job for you, Paul," Quinten said. "Go down to the Security Officer and tell him I want my order passed to every officer and noncom in charge of a team. Some of them won't have heard the speakers. Also, I suppose you'd better welcome the commanding officer of the troops. I don't know what rank he'll be. Bring him right up here."

Howard looked carefully at Quinten. The general seemed calm now, and at peace. He wondered for a moment whether he ought to leave Quinten alone. Then he realised it didn't matter much. Quinten had the gun. There was nothing he could do to stop Quinten taking any action he thought fit. From somewhere on the base a long burst of machine-gun fire shattered the quiet. Men were still dying out there, Howard told himself. They would continue to die until they received the orders to end the fight.

He nodded stiffly and turned away. At the door he paused. "General," he said awkwardly, "you're sure you'll be all right?"

Quinten smiled. It was a genuine, warm smile, the

kind of smile Howard hadn't seen on Quinten's face for a long time. "I'll be fine, Paul. Just fine. Get those orders out fast."

"I'll get them out fast." Howard went out through the door. Quinten watched him go. He heard the noise of his steps in the corridor, and the slam of the door which cut off the two command offices from the rest of the building. He thought Howard was a good boy. In time he'd make a real good commander, too.

Quinten moved over to the door. It was two minutes after the deadline he had set himself. He carefully locked the door, and went back to his desk. A year, the specialist had said. Maybe as little as six months. Maybe as much as two years. How wrong could a man be?

From the second drawer of his left hand pedestal he took a slim wallet of photographs. He looked at them for a few moments, then replaced them in the wallet and put the wallet back in the drawer. On the desk in front of him the heavy, lethal bulk of the four five was like a magnet, drawing his attention to it as it lay across the closed cover of his note pad. He felt an urge to pick it up to feel in his hand again the heft of the familiar weapon. He fought the urge down. As he had told Howard, he believed he would have to account for what he had done. There were certain formalities. They did not detain him long.

Within minutes of leaving Quinten's office, Howard had ensured that the orders to cease fire were in course of transmission to all defence teams. He met the commander of the attacking troops, a short, lively light colonel, saluted him as courtesy demanded, and escorted him up to Quinten's office.

He tapped on Quinten's door. It was the first time he had done that since he acquired the exec's privilege of free entry. There was no reply. He tapped again, and a third time. Still no reply.

The door was tough. It took them nearly a minute before they succeeded in kicking it open. Howard was first into the room. It didn't help at all that he expected what he saw. The wave of nausea lasted all of thirty seconds, and then it was gone and he was ready to start work again.

While the infantry colonel stood by him, he initiated action to trace Bailey and Hudson. Pretty soon he knew the answer. Wherever they were, they were not on Sonora Base.

THE PENTAGON

11.30 G.M.T.
Moscow: 2.30 p.m.
Washington: 6.30 a.m.

IN WASHINGTON the first pale light of an early dawn was appearing in the Eastern sky. In Moscow, the streets were gloomy with the approach of a winter dusk. Between the two cities the invisible radio links hummed and crackled with the passage of new information between the Russian and American staffs, and occasionally a short exchange between the President and the Marshal himself.

Most of the bombers of the 843rd were over Russian territory now. The intersections plotted on their tracks, which represented another five minutes flying towards their targets, were creeping steadily onwards and inwards, so that the map now resembled nothing more than a series of railway lines, all slowly moving into the Russian interior, as each five minutes a sleeper was laid across the track to indicate progress.

One of the tracks ended in a small red cross just south of Kxyl Orda in Turkestan. The Russians had reported the destruction of a B-52 at that point. They had been reticent about the method of destruction, merely that the bomber had exploded in the air. The bombs had not been detonated.

Intelligence had deduced from this that the 52 had had the misfortune to cross an experimental missile area. They knew already that the Russians used certain areas of the Kizil Kum desert to test missiles, and had fired some of their early intermediate range missiles from the Kizil Kum as targets in the Aral Sea.

The news had been brought straight in to General Steele, just as he was about to sum up the overall situation. He glanced at the report, frowned, and began to speak. "Mr. President, Your Excellency, the air situation is this. The eight forty-third is steadily moving in on its targets, and although some of the airplanes have now been over Russian territory for a considerable period, we have received only two reports of them being engaged and hit. The first reported a hit on a bomber flying south towards Kolguev. We have now established that this bomber's primary target is the I.C.B.M. Base at Kotlass. We do not know whether the plane is still flying or not. We are counting it as probably destroyed.

"We feel on safe ground in counting it as probably destroyed since news has just come of another bomber which has been definitely destroyed I am glad to say"—he glanced briefly at Zorubin—"that the bombs did not explode, and as far as we know no casualties were caused except to the crew of the plane."

"Thank you," Zorubin said quietly.

"This incident occurred in an area where we know there to be a Russian experimental missile centre. I refer to the Kizil Kum desert, Your Excellency."

Zorubin nodded his head. "You are correct."

"There is a parallel between the two incidents in that both have occurred in areas where the bombers were likely to encounter experimental missiles. On the other hand, none of the other bombers seem to have been hit. We are now becoming certain that the normal Russian missile and fighter defences are not going to be able to stop the 52.K's. We may lose two or three more. The majority will get through.

"As regards enemy air, there are no reports yet of the Soviet bomber force taking off. There is more activity than usual on the light bomber airfields facing NATO, but so far no positive indication that an attack is intended. Sixth Fleet reports it is being shadowed by two submarines. Admiral Maclellan feels this is part of the normal procedure the Russians follow since they got access to Egyptian and Syrian bases. As far as Sixth Fleet is concerned, shadowing by Russian subs is S.O.P. They aren't worried about it. From all other sea areas reports are of normalcy, no hostile contacts whatsoever have been reported.

"From all this, Mr. President, we have reached two firm conclusions. Disregarding political probabilities, we feel sure the Russians cannot get their long range bombers off the ground fast enough before their fields are smeared. And secondly, that at least twenty-eight of the bombers will penetrate to their targets."

"I see." The President was thoughtful. "Assuming twenty-five only get through, would they deal a mortal blow?"

"I wouldn't say mortal," Franklin answered quckly. "It's a big country. Crippling would be a better expression. It would leave them completely at the mercy of any forces which followed up, because they wouldn't have the strength left to hit those forces where it counts, that is on the bases back in this country. Their offensive power would be so badly weakened I doubt whether they'd succeed in getting more than two or three bombs on to this country."

"And they'd realise that?"

"Well, yes, Mr. President, they would. Any competent air staff could work out the answer in ten minutes."

"I must know whether a further blow is being contemplated if you cannot succeed in recalling your bombers." Zorubin's voice was harsh. The President glanced at him in surprise. The Russian Ambassador's face had lost its usually ruddy colour. It was pale, and the expression in Zorubin's eyes was desperate.

"It is not," he said flatly. He thought that Zorubin must know of the existence of the world-killing devices buried in the Urals. He revised his estimate of Zorubin's importance. To have that information, the Russian would have to be very close to the central power.

General Keppler picked up his telephone in response to the winking light. He listened for a few moments, and then said, "O.K., get in to the commander's office fast. Don't waste a second." He replaced the phone. "Commander at Sonora's ceased fire," he said briefly. "I've instructed Mackenzie, the battalion commander, to get to Quinten's office the fastest he can."

"Yes," the President said. "Very good." The wall clock showed eleven thirty-six. The sands were running out fast now, too fast. "Steele," he asked, "supposing we get the correct code group, how long is it going to take to get the word out to the bombers?"

"Two or three minutes," Steele said confidently. "At the maximum."

"So if we got the group by, say, twelve hundred hours, we could still prevent the attack?"

"Well, not really," Franklin interposed. "It's true the *average* bomb time for the wing is a few minutes after twelve. But there's a period allowed each side of the bomb time, four minutes actually. Some of the bombers would bomb exactly two hours after turning from their X points. Probably most of them would try to bomb at the earliest possible time. That's only natural, they wouldn't want to prolong the flight any longer than they had to. I would say the big majority of the crews, when they turned in at ten hundred, planned on two hours to bomb time."

"I see." The President showed no trace of discomposure, but he was beginning to feel an increasing certainty that they would not be able to recall the bombers now. Quinten's planning had been first class, he thought. The 843rd was going to catch the Russian bombers before they could get off. Or at least before they could get off fully armed and briefed. Everything was working out as Quinten had probably calculated it. He couldn't believe that the general would have slipped up by allowing officers who were present at the briefing to remain on the base. The last hope now was that when Quinten heard the President's information about the devices which threatened the whole world, he would grasp quickly that he must allow his bombers to be recalled.

The light on Keppler's phone glowed. Keppler snatched it up. "Mackenzie? Sure, Keppler here. He what? . . . Sure, I get it . . . They aren't? . . . Well look for them, goddam it .. Yeah, we'll keep a line open to you." He slammed the phone back on its rest.

"Well, what did he say? Have they found the officers?" Zorubin's voice was high pitched, frightened.

"Quinten has shot himself," Keppler said heavily. "No-one knows where the two officers who attended the briefing are. Their wives say they left on a hunting trip last night, and there seems no reason to doubt that. They're looking for them, but Mackenzie doesn't sound hopeful they'll find them."

"*Bogou moiou!*" Zorubin's face was a deathly white. "Then it is finished. Everything is finished." He lit a cigarette with hands that shook badly as he applied a match to the tobacco.

The President thought for a moment. So the last hope had gone. At the back of his mind from the first had lurked the fear that Quinten might kill himself when he saw he would be taken. It was logical, and if Quinten had been sick enough to believe in his original action, then he would not have hesitated to do anything in order to ensure his action continued. Now it was necessary to communicate the news to Moscow. He turned and spoke for a short while to the Secretary of State. Then he said to Zorubin, "I'm going to talk to the Marshal again."

The president spoke quickly and simply. He told the Marshal that it seemed all efforts to recall the bombers had failed. They would go on trying, but he did not think they would succeed.

"*Sookin Sin!*" The President winced as the coarse obscenity crashed from the speaker. He listened in silence to a torrent of Russian lasting half a minute or more.

"Murderers," Zorubin translated. His voice was filled with fear, causing him to stumble over words, and mispronounce others. There was no trace now of the cultured elegance which normally characterized his English. "Swinish aggressors. You have launched an unprovoked attack on a peaceful country. Up to now I have kept my bomber force on the ground. I have refrained from any action which might be thought to be warlike. But now you will pay. The Soviet people will take their just vengeance on the capitalist imperialist murderers."

The President said calmly, "We acknowledged our fault. We have done all we can to stop it. We supplied enough warning for the cities to be evacuated and the people saved. Let the Marshal consider that if his Government had ever ceased their world-wide aggression, this would never have happened. For years they have forced a terrible economic strain upon us so that we might have weapons to defend ourselves against an attack which he knows he has planned. Not only our economy has been strained, but our minds and our nerves. Now, one of our commanders has reached breaking point. Would the Marshal deny that his own acts of aggression have contributed to the commander's breakdown? But this is no time for an exchange of insults. We must consider what we can yet do. Your cities will be destroyed, or a few of them, but most of the targets are not near cities. You have no doubt evacuated your cities, so loss of life should not be high. For the damage we do, we will pay. We will pay, even though it reduces us to economic poverty. That is only right. We can promise there will be little radio-active fall-out from the bombs. Let the Marshal remember that all is not yet lost. And I repeat my solemn promise. For whatever damage is done, we will pay."

There was silence in the room while the President's speech was translated at the other end of the radio link, thousands of miles away. A minute went by. The President thought he had never known a longer one. Then the speaker crackled with two short, sharply spoken sentences, and was silent.

Zorubin's voice was empty of hope. "You couldn't afford it," he translated. "But you will certainly pay." He turned to face the President. "It is the end," he said resignedly. "I can tell it from his voice."

"You know him so well?" the President asked.

"He is my oldest friend," Zorubin said simply. "If those targets are destroyed he will be a man without power, a man who has been defeated. He will not endure that. He will take certain action. I do not know whether even now I should tell you . . ."

The President interrupted him. "We know," he said. "We know about the devices in the Urals."

"So? But perhaps you do not know for certain if they would be used?"

"My guess," the President said slowly, "is they will."

Zorubin nodded. "You are right, they will. And you know what it means?"

"We do."

"So that is it." Zorubin shrugged. His face was slowly returning to its normal colour. There it was again, the President thought, the peculiarly Slav acceptance of fate.

"You know, Mr. President," Zorubin said almost lightly, "a little while ago General Franklin said that when the planes turned in from their X points there was two hours to bomb time. I can put it more accurately than that. Not just two hours to bomb time. But two hours to doom."

"ALABAMA ANGEL"

11.35 G.M.T.
Moscow: 2.35 p.m.
Washingon: 6.35 a.m.

THE GRIM roll call was over. The bodies of Goldsmith, Minter, and Mellows, had been laid on the floor of the cabin near the rear bulkhead. Each of the surviving crew members had thought for a few brief seconds about the dead men, then got back to work and the difficult job of getting the bomber to the position where it could avenge their deaths and the deaths of millions more back home.

Maybe the dead were lucky, Brown thought. At least they did not have to carry the shapeless weight of pain whose torturing fingers were pressing ever heavier on his back. They did not have to carry the responsibility of taking a crippled bomber in to its bomb point, and muster the determination to get there, which alone would enable the heavy odds against success to be beaten.

Determination. That was what counted now. If he could concentrate hard enough, long enough, he would get *Alabama Angel* to the target. Maybe, if he concentrated sufficiently hard, his mind would conquer the rolling waves of pain which urged him ceaselessly to seek the easy refuge of a morphia ampoule from the first aid pack. He gazed ahead at the white blur of snow a few hundred feet below, following the slight rises and falls of the ground, knowing his radio altimeter would flash a brilliant red if he went below the four hundred feet altitude he had set on it.

Survival depended on staying low now. At this height the bomber could not be tracked by radar, or so the intelligence reports insisted. Well, they'd been right about most things. They couldn't be blamed for the missile ship marooned out there in the ice of the Barents Sea. If radar couldn't track the bomber, it couldn't control fighters in to intercept and attack. And missiles fired from the ground would be completely ineffective with the bomber at this height.

There were three things might stop the bomber penetrating to the target, he thought. A fighter which picked them up haphazardly, without benefit of radar control. Fast firing light weapons sited to defend targets against low level attack. And, ever present, the danger he might not see an obstacle in time, or that the radio altimeter would suddenly fail to function.

Weapons sited to defend against low level attack he dismissed easily. Kotlass was out of range of the fighter bombers on the N.A.T.O. airfields. A long range bomber like the 52 would never come in at low level. *Alabama Angel* was coming in low level, but that was one of those things. It was quite unintentional. And you couldn't plan for the unintentional as well as the intentional tactics in war.

Fighters operating independently of radar control were a slightly bigger threat. They would have scrambled every available all-weather fighter on freelance patrols. It was quite possible one or more of those fighters would pick the bomber up. But Brown remembered how a friend of his, who was the pilot of an all-weather F.104, had described the task of intercepting a fast moving bomber only a few hundred feet above the ground at night. *"Ape sweat,"* the friend said flatly. There were too many factors against the fighter. Bad visibility, poor radar response, danger from the bomber's jet wash, were just a few of them. Brown's friend had put the chances of successful interception under those conditions at about one in twenty.

The glaring red light of his radio altimeter blazed in the darkness of the cabin. Brown pulled back on the stick, instantly realising he had been deceived by a gentle upward slope of the ground. The red light disappeared, and he eased forward again before the green winked on. He had set the altimeter so it showed red below four hundred, green above five. In the hundred feet between those heights lay safety for *Alabama Angel.* But the danger of flying into the ground, or an obstacle in the path of the bomber, remained the greatest of the threats. His concentration had to be absolute. He said, "How many miles to the target, Stan? And how many minutes?"

"I'll let you know shortly," Andersen said. "Engelbach, keep looking for a big river ahead of us. We should cross it around three minutes from now. Ninety degrees to our track."

"Would that be the Peza?"

"Yeah," Andersen said. "It would." You stupid bastard, he thought, what the hell else would it be? The Dnieper? He checked himself, pulling back the momentary anger that had blazed in him. Engelbach was like that. But he was thorough, and he didn't make mistakes. "Try and give me an accurate pinpoint when we cross," he went on. His voice was quiet and friendly.

"Sure, Stan," Engelbach said. "I'll get you a pinpoint."

"Captain?" It was Garcia's voice.

Brown wriggled in his seat, trying to ease the sticky wetness he could feel between himself and the fabric. The movement sent a fresh spasm of pain through him. He shuddered, said tightly, "Garcia?"

"Captain, I have to know about the bombs. What height you going to bomb?"

"Twenty thousand."

"O.K., so I'll have to alter the fusing. Otherwise, we drop it and the safety plugs come out, it'll go off right away."

"Yes." Brown worked on the problem for a moment. What Garcia said made sense. As the bombs dropped away from the plane the last safety devices were made inoperative. If a bomb was fused to blast at twenty thousand feet it would do so, regardless of the bomber a few feet above it. Maybe a delay would do the trick. He said: "If you fuse for ground level, what's the maximum delay?"

"Forty seconds."

Brown calculated quickly. It should be enough. If he turned away right after the bomb was released he should be at least ten miles away when it exploded. The blast wouldn't destroy as great a ground area as a fused air burst, but it would do the job. He said, "All right, Garcia. Fuse number one for ground level. Put in full delay. I don't figure we'll be able to make the secondary. Remove the trigger primer from number two and check it's safe. We'll jettison it when we cross out again."

"Will do," Garcia said. "I'll report when I've finished, Captain."

"O.K., Garcia. How's the leg?"

"I'll live," Garcia said lightly. He moved over to begin the delicate process of re-fusing one bomb, unarming the other. His leg wasn't hurting too badly. He had shot it full of novocain from a first aid pack. Maybe it was against the rules, but the rules had never bothered him. Not like Minter's sightless gaze did now. He leaned over and gently pulled the eyelids down over the dead eyes. Then he went to work.

Brown said, "Bill, take a look at Mellows' set. Maybe it's still working. I'd like to get an attack message off when the time comes."

"O.K., Captain." Lieutenant Owens pushed his way past Federov to Meadows' position.

"River coming up," Engelbach said sharply. "Crossing, crossing, *now*."

Andersen glanced at the chronometer, quickly noted the time on his log. Now, if Engelbach had got an accurate pin point, he could navigate.

Engelbach said, "Stan, I'm near enough sure we cross at square H, one five four, two zero five. On the target approach chart."

"Fine," Andersen slid an approach transparency over his chart, plotted in Engelbach's figures. "It looks about right," he said slowly. "Not far off track. Next thing to look for is a town just to starboard, in about six minutes. Ivanovsk. That's the name, no kidding. Small town, about the size of—" Andersen hesitated He had been about to say Dothan, Alabama. He went on quickly, "Well, a small town. Then a minute after that you should see where the Vashka river joins the Mezen. I'd like another pinpoint as we cross the Mezen."

"I'll get it," Engelbach said confidently. His radar wasn't much use at this height. But he hadn't forgotten the map reading principles he'd learned. Even at this speed, when he knew what to look for and at what time, he could usually pick it out. He marked the time he should expect the pinpoint on his map, and stared out ahead at the white countryside.

Brown had heard the exchanges between Andersen and Engelbach only faintly. He was aware that more and more, when he was not himself receiving information or giving orders, he was concentrating on the flying of the bomber to the exclusion of all else. Maybe, he thought, it was an automatic process. His body knew it had not the strength to participate in everything. It saved itself for the important times. Someone was calling him through the intercom. He forced himself to listen, and to accept the message. It was Garcia, telling him number one bomb had been re-fused, number two made safe.

Then there was Andersen's voice. But the navigator's message missed him. He said weakly, "Again, Stan."

Andersen detected the weakness and pain in Brown's voice. He said, "Clint, listen to me. Clint, you hear me?"

"Sure." Brown summoned up reserves of strength, fighting desperately against the blackness which was slowly engulfing him. Suddenly it receded. He felt new strength flood into his tired, agonised body. The pain eased a little.

"Clint, you O.K.?" Andersen's voice was high pitched, anxious.

"I'm O.K. What's the word?"

"Alter course three degrees port. Estimate twelve zero nine

at target. We've got a high tail wind down here. You got that, Clint? Set it on your count-down. Twenty-six minutes to run to target."

"Roger. Altering course now." Brown went through the motions mechanically. He altered course, set the count-down time, found a few seconds to ponder just what performance they'd built into this plane. Admittedly the six remaining engines were full out. Sure, they were burning fuel at a fantastic rate. But what the hell. The bomber was going in at a speed not far off sound. They knew how to build them at Seattle.

He knew there was something about Seattle. It worried him. Seattle. Why should it worry him now? There was something, but it didn't matter. The target did. They'd want to know back home when he'd taken it out. He said, "Owens, how's the radio?"

"Well, I'm not radio expert. It got hit, but the CRM 114 took most of the impact. The transmitter seems O.K., but the receiver's out. There's no current coming through to it."

"All right, you stay there. You know enough morse to get off the attack signal." Brown peered ahead of him, looking past the redness that was trying to push itself in front of his eyes. "The receiver doesn't matter now. There's nothing anyone would want to tell us we don't already know."

SONORA, TEXAS

11.40 G.M.T.
Moscow: 2.40 p.m.
Washington: 6.40 a.m.

LIEUTENANT COLONEL Andrew Mackenzie, who had led the attack on Sonora, replaced the telephone. "They don't like it," he said. "They don't like it one little bit. I told them there was still a chance the two officers were on the base somewhere, but if they aren't at their quarters and their wives say they went off hunting, it looks hopeless to me. I suppose there's a chance the whirlybirds might locate them."

Howard looked out at the brilliantly lit base. Every possible light had been turned on, to help the ambulances and the medics locate and care for the casualties. As he watched, an ambulance tore across the concrete, siren howling and red light flashing. It disappeared in the direction of the base hospital. Here and there, groups of walking wounded were being assembled to receive their shots while they waited for ambulances. In the distance, on the broad concrete of the 739th servicing area, men were bending over sprawling figures which would never stand again, and covering them with G.I. blankets.

Howard thought about Bailey and Hudson. They were fanatically keen hunters. They were probably dug in right now in an elaborate hide somewhere a hundred miles away from Sonora, possibly near the coast, waiting for the dawn rise of birds. They had their own favourite places, as all hunters did, and like most hunters they kept it a close secret between themselves. Three whirlybirds had already gone off. Howard watched the fourth rise out of sight, into the darkness above the airfield where the lights did not penetrate. "There's a chance," he said. "About one in a million. Bailey and Hudson might be anywhere in ten thousand square smiles, and it won't be light for a long while yet."

Mackenzie joined Howard at the window. "It was pretty bad out there," he said quietly. "Those flak towers are hell to pass without artillery support."

"Yeah. You know what all this is about?"

"Well," Mackenzie said cautiously. "The poop is the general here went haywire and mounted a full-scale attack on Russia. Our orders to penetrate here came right from the President. Incidentally, they're keeping a line open from this office to the Pentagon, in case we locate those guys."

"I don't get it," Howard muttered. "Maybe Quinten's action was wrong, but it's done now. Seems to me the only sensible thing is to follow up on it. Why the hell would they want to sacrifice all those poor bastards out there?"

Mackenzie shrugged. "Don't ask me, I'm just a footslogger. It's you guys are all mixed up in the big bomb diplomacy. I heard some more poop from the Pentagon. The officer who passed me my orders used to be my divisional commander. The word is the Reds have a super bomb can wreck the whole of the States."

"Nuts," Howard said angrily. "And even if they did, how could they deliver it? We've caught them off balance, Colonel. Quinten may have been sick, but he still knew which end was up when it came to bomber operations. Understand, I'm not defending what he did. Fifteen minutes ago I was beginning to think he was right. Now, I'm not sure. But I do know he wouldn't miscalculate the effect of his attack."

"Well, I hope you're right." Mackenzie pursed his thin lips thoughtfully. "Seems to me someone up top must know something more, though. I don't know the exact figures yet, but I must have lost near on two hundred of my boys in that attack. What did you lose?"

"We don't know. Certainly over a hundred."

"That's three hundred men gone, at the minimum. They must figure the position to be pretty serious when they'll accept casualties like that." He turned away and walked to the door. "Well, I'm going out to see how my boys are doing. Have to take a muster to count just who's left." He closed the door quietly behind him.

Howard still stood at the window, lost in thought. Some time in the next few minutes two medics entered with a stretcher. Howard looked out at the base while they removed what was left of Quinten, and cleared up some of the mess. When a man puts a four five in his mouth and pulls the trigger, there is inevitably a mess.

He heard the medics leave, and he caught sight of Mackenzie's slim, energetic figure moving among the troops. Then he turned to the desk.

The medics had removed the gun from the desk, but Quinten's note pad still lay there. Howard sat down in Quinten's seat, and idly flicked the pages of the pad. Quinten had found peace now, he thought. Maybe not peace on earth, but peace wherever he had gone to.

It was funny, he thought, flipping the pages and glancing idly at the scrawls and doodles there, how much of a man's subconscious is revealed when he scrawls on a pad. His conscious mind may be busy with other things. But his subconscious often prompts him to scrawl thoughts which are hidden deep beneath the surface. Here was his own name, he saw. But Quinten had promoted him. He had gone up to light colonel. Howard smiled sourly. After this mess he'd be lucky if he stayed a major. Here was Kotlass, with the K heavily underlined. A double connection there. The I.C.B.M.

site, with the K underlined from the bombers heading towards it to take it out. He turned over another page.

Suddenly he stiffened in his seat. He riffed hastily through the other pages. Yes, there it was again. And again. Howard felt his heart pounding heavily with excitement. He thought he knew. No, stronger than that, he was *sure* he knew.

He stretched out his hand to pick up the telephone with a line held to the Pentagon. Then instantly he saw and heard Quinten again, his face haggard and pale, but his voice calm, and confident and utterly reasonable. He hesitated. *The mongoose kills the snake. He does it because that is the nature of things. It is not aggression, it is self defence. We will bury you, the Russians said. We will bury you.* He pulled his hand back, stood, and walked slowly to the window.

In his mind reason pitted itself against morality, hard fact against probability. He was sure he had the power to recall the bombers. He was not sure he should exercise that power. He lit a cigarette and glanced at the wall clock. Eleven forty-six. Whatever his decision, it had to be fast.

Two hundred yards away from his window he saw an ambulance pull up alongside a group of wounded. The medics bent over the stretchers, lifting them smoothly into the ambulance. He watched as a stretcher was brought to the ambulance, and two men bent over it. Even at that distance he saw quite clearly that one of the men shook his head. The stretcher was taken away, and put back on the concrete. Someone walked over and placed a blanket over the still load.

Howard knew then what he had to do. He didn't believe the story about the super bomb. That was just the politicians pressing the panic button again. Nor did he believe the attack on Sonora had been motivated by anything much more than an attempt to conciliate world opinion. But he had just seen a man die. Not a mongoose, or a cobra, but a man. That was where Quinten was wrong. It was all right for animals to kill by instinct. It was all wrong for men to kill except in direct self defence. Nothing could justify it. He crossed to the desk and picked up the telephone. For a few moments he had held the fate of the world in his hands. But he did not know that. He only knew that he could see what was right, and he had to act in accordance with what he saw.

The connection with the Pentagon was almost immediate. His call was answered by a colonel whose name was unfamiliar. "Pass your message, Major," the colonel said.

Howard took a deep breath. "I'll pass it to the President," he said firmly. "No-one else."

He braced himself for a storm of angry words from the other end. But they did not come. Instead, there was a moment's silence, and then a new voice said, "Major Howard? This is General Steele, Chief of Staff. You can pass your message to me, son."

Howard hesitated. This was the big brass. If he bucked it his career was finished for sure. But he stuck to his guns. "General, I'm sorry, sir," he said. "I don't recognise your voice. I think I have the recall code group for the eight forty-third, but I insist on passing it to the President personally. I'll know his voice all right."

Again Howard was surprised by the response. General Steele said nothing more than, "Hold on son, I'll get him."

Howard felt an intense nervousness come over him as he waited. He'd stuck his neck right out now. He'd insisted on direct access to someone outside of the proper military channels. His military sense of fitness was outraged, yet his common sense insisted he was right.

He heard a few faint noises in the background, and then a voice he knew was speaking to him. The tones were quiet, precise, cultured. He identified them instantly. The voice said, "This is the President, Major. General Steel tells me you might have the recall group for the eight forty-third wing. You may pass it to me."

Howard found his nervousness had left him. There was something about the voice had given him confidence and assurance. He began to speak.

" ALABAMA ANGEL "

11.45 G.M.T.
Moscow: 2.45 p.m.
Washington: 6.45 a.m.

Lieutenant Stan Andersen was satisfied. The new course was working out fine, taking them in a straight line to the target. He laid his pencil down and said, "Clint."

"Yes, Stan?"

"How're you doing? Anything I can get you?"

"I'm making out," Brown said quietly. "Don't worry about me, I'm not hit bad." The pain was less savage now, or maybe he was more used to it. It didn't worry him nearly so much as the numbness which was gradually moving up his back and into his shoulders. He knew he was getting weaker, that his reserves of strength were fast being expended. Well, in another half hour or so it wouldn't matter. Federov could take over, and he could sleep. He was beginning to feel very tired.

"That's great," Andersen said. But he wasn't too sure. He'd seen the mess the fragment had made of Brown's clothing, and the wide area soaked with blood. He went on, "Shouldn't need any alteration in course now. Estimate twelve zero eight at target. We've been lucky, there's a dandy of a tail wind. Engelbach, you can take her in on visual and target radar. We start climbing at twelve hundred exactly, so you'll have about five minutes after reaching height to pick up the aiming point and make corrections before you let her go. O.K.?"

"O.K., Stan," Engelbach said. He arranged in order the series of strip maps prepared for just such an eventuality as a bomber having to run the last two hundred or so miles to target at low level. Ordinary maps were little use at this height. The low level strip maps showed only the prominent landmarks, one every three minutes flight. From these the bombardier could make the small corrections which might be necessary to keep the bomber heading straight in. The first of the landmarks was the Pinega River as it flowed across the track from east to west, and the next the same river nearer its source flowing west to east. He looked out ahead into the white blur of the approaching landscape.

Ahead of *Alabama Angel* a dozen red flames appeared, coming down from above, getting further away and lower, moving much faster than the bomber. They exploded on the ground, a vivid cluster of brilliant flashes. Seconds later the bomber flew over the point where the explosions had occurred, and rocked in the violently churning air they had left.

"Rockets," Brown said quietly.

"There he goes, overshooting to port." Andersen, now he had finished navigating, had his head up in the astrodome. "Looks like a delta-wing type. See him, Clint?"

Brown had caught the merest glimpse of a slim delta-wing shape, black against the surrounding whiteness. "I think so," he said cautiously. "Think he's coming in again?"

"I lost him. He aimed off too high on that one."

"Yeah," Brown said. There was an intolerable itching in his left foot. He tried to wriggle the toes of the foot, and found he couldn't move them. Then he tried to move the whole foot. Again, no response. He realised his left leg had died on him, and he began to have an idea just how badly he'd been hit. He thought for a moment that he'd conceal it from the rest of the crew. But that was futile. If he passed out without warning at this height they'd be into the deck in less than a second. He said, "Federov."

"Captain?"

"Federov, I want you to stand by my seat. Keep watching me. If I look like going forward, haul her up higher fast until you can drag me out. You understand?"

"Sure," Federov said. He moved forward to stand beside Brown.

"Clint, you're hit bad." Andersen's voice was urgent. "How do you feel?"

"I'll make it." With the assertion Brown's confidence returned. It had wavered for a few moments. Now it was strong again. He'd make it because he had to. He'd hit the target because the target just had to be hit. It was as easy as that.

"Fighter," Andersen shouted. He had picked out the dark blur as it dived, lost it momentarily, then seen the red flare as it fired its rockets. This cluster hit a half mile behind *Alabama Angel*. One or two strays carried further, but the nearest was two to three hundred yards behind the bomber. Seconds later the black delta shape flashed by above them.

"My God," Engelbach said. "Solid wall of flak ahead. Maybe five miles. Man, it's solid. No space to squeeze through."

Brown looked out ahead, lifting his gaze from the point of ground a mile ahead of the bomber he had been concentrating on.

Englebach was right, he thought. It was a wall. As far as he could see ahead the sky was criss-crossed with arcing lines of tracer, laced with hundreds of small explosions. He looked quickly to port and starboard. The flak wall seemed to extend without limit in both directions.

Suddenly there was a bigger explosion among the lines of tracer. Something glowed, showered out flame, dropped swiftly to earth and exploded. It could have been the fighter which had just made the attack. Brown thought. Pilot probably concentrating on instruments, never even saw it. He said quickly, "What do you make of it, Stan?"

"Looked like they hit an airplane. Maybe the same fighter just tried to take us out."

"Yeah," Brown said, "but I didn't mean that. You think we should go through. Or try to get round it. Or maybe go over the top?"

"I wouldn't think it was any use trying to go round it. They've probably got Kotlass ringed in. It's their number one target, the highest of all priority ones. To go over it is out. That's what it's there for, to force a low level attacker up where the fighters can get at him with a certain chance of hitting him."

"So we go through," Brown said calmly. He reached forward and adjusted his radio altimeter for two hundred feet. "I'm going right down on the deck. Anything gets us at two hundred feet will be a real lucky shot. Any more speed in hand, Federov?"

Federov shook his head no. "Nothing more," he said sourly. "Not a single, lousy knot. We're stretched out full now."

"Yeah, I figured that." It was funny, Brown thought, the way the Russians could afford the number of guns to ring a place like Kotlass, still two hundred miles away. He began to figure out the number of guns it would require, then gave the effort up as useless. He only knew it was a hell of a lot.

"How far you make it now?" he asked.

"Guess I underestimated," Engelbach said. "Must have been more than five miles. The target radar shows the first concentration about two now."

"O.K." Brown said easily. He brought the big plane down to two hundred. Ten seconds to go. He hunched a little in his seat, purely instinctively. The movement brought a vicious, unexpected stab of pain. For a moment he almost wished the bomber would be caught right away in the flak. Then the pain would be over. But as it subsided into a heavy but bearable ache he forgot it and concentrated on the delicately precise job of flying the airplane at the ridiculous height of two hundred feet.

In the cold air the lazy arcs of tracer glowed with a white incandescence. They crossed and re-crossed in a graceful, lethal pattern. Here and there the sudden bright red eruptions of explosions were quickly born and as quickly died. Brown forgot his wound, the pain, the numbness which was penetrating inside his shoulder muscles now, in the determination to break through the wall. Maybe it was like the sonic barrier. Maybe, once it was broken, there was smooth air, and quiet, and easy passage. Or maybe it continued all the way to the target. Brown tapped his last reservoirs of energy, and poured his strength into the concentration needed to burst through the flak.

And *Alabama Angel*, so low as to be almost sliding along the ground, hurled herself at the last obstacle between her and her fulfilment, which was the I.C.B.M. base at Kotlass.

THE PENTAGON

11.50 G.M.T.
Moscow: 2.50 p.m.
Washington: 6.50 a.m.

THERE WAS little conversation in the room within the War Room. Since the unconcealed threat by the Marshal, nothing more had come over the air from Moscow. Twice, the President had tried to re-establish personal contact. But the speakers in the room had remained ominously silent.

Steele had reported that there were still no positive signs that the Soviet bomber force was taking the air. Franklin felt a passing regret that Quinten's plan, which had succeeded beyond all possible doubt, would mean only annihilation for everyone, not the brilliant victory it deserved. Somehow it did not make sense to forge a weapon of the finest metal, temper it to an infinite hardness, polish it to a dazzling perfection, only to find that it could not in any case be employed without destroying its wielder as surely as the enemy it struck down. Well, he thought, that was the twentieth century. They had to live with it. Or rather, he amended, to die with it.

The intelligence colonel came in to report another bomber destroyed. Again the destruction had occurred in an area known to be allocated to the testing of experimental missiles. Three down, but twenty-nine still flying on, most of them only ten minutes away from their targets now.

Zorubin broke the gloomy silence. "How long will we have?" he asked.

"Six weeks, possibly. Perhaps a little less, perhaps a little more. We will of course provide transportation for you to return to Russia, if you wish it."

Zorubin shook his head. "No, Mr. President, I think not. I have no ties in Russia. Most of my life I have passed outside it. I think I will stay here in Washington. It has occurred to me now I no longer have to live a life of the utmost decorum, I can perhaps accept some of the invitations certain of your ladies have hinted they would be happy to extend to me. On the average, they are much more attractive than our Russian women," he continued reflectively. "Excessive concentration on political and economic theory may produce a well informed woman. It certainly produces a dull one, from the point of sexual attraction, don't you think?"

"No doubt," the President said stiffly. He could understand Zorubin's attitude, especially when one considered that Zorubin had already accepted and rationalised the fact he must inevitably die. But he could not sympathise with it.

"Eat, drink, and be merry," Zorubin said lightly. "I remember a wily old British diplomat in London who . . ." he broke off as the call light of General Steele's phone flickered.

Steele picked up his phone and listened. "Put him through," he said sharply. "Right away." He waited a few moments, then said, "Major Howard? This is General Steele, Chief of Staff. You can pass your message to me, son." He listened for the reply. Then he said, "Hold on son, I'll get him."

Steele laid down the phone. "Mr. President," he said quietly. "The exec at Sonora thinks he knows the recall group. He'll only pass it to you personally. Shall I get him switched through to your phone?"

The President was already standing. "No," he said quickly, "I'll come to yours." He moved swiftly round the table. Even with the best run switchboard, calls sometimes got lost when they were switched from one extension to another. One small error by an operator now could mean the difference between life and extinction. He accepted the phone from Steele, and took a deep breath.

"This is the President, Major," he said. "General Steele tells me you might have the recall group for the eight forty-third wing. You may pass it to me."

At Sonora, Paul Howard felt no trace of nervousness. "I don't know whether I'm right, sir," he said clearly, "but I think I am. You see, sir, General Quinten was talking a lot to me in the last couple of hours. And most of the time he was doodling on his notepad."

The President interrupted quietly. "Keep telling me about it, Major, but first, right or wrong, give me the code letters. Even seconds count now."

"Sir, I think they will be some combination of the letters O, P, and E."

"I'll repeat those," the President said. "Some combination of O, P, and E." He spoke clearly and slowly. Out of the corner of his eye he saw Franklin take off at a run for the door. The wall clock showed five minutes to twelve. He felt a wild excitement mounting in him. Maybe they'd save the world yet. "Now, carry on, Major."

"Well, sir, General Quinten explained to me just how he saw the attack he'd ordered. He saw it as the only possible way to stop an attack on this country he was sure was coming. He figured that all the factors needed for success were present, and the eight forty-third would be able to destroy Russian offensive strength. If things worked out the way he calculated them, he thought this country would not receive any damage. Obviously he must have miscalculated somewhere."

"No," the President said. "He didn't miscalculate. His plan, as far as it went, has worked out with complete success.

He didn't miscalculate on the information he had, but his information wasn't complete."

"Then there was a good reason why this base was attacked?"

"A very good reason."

"Oh," Howard said. "I figured there had to be. Anyway, after telling me how it would work, Quinten explained *why* he had taken the action. His reasons sounded pretty convincing to me. They boiled down to the fact if we didn't destroy the Russians now, they would certainly destroy us in the next year or so. He said the only way we could ensure peace was to kill them now. He told me a story about some mongoose breaking a cobra's eggs to illustrate what he meant."

"Rikki-tikki-tavi," the President murmured.

"Yes, sir, that was the name. The general kept talking about peace, and he used the expression *peace on earth* at least twice. Once when he asked me what the sound of a SAC wing going off really meant, and once when he said the men he was allowing to die on the airfield were dying for that.

"After the medics had taken his body away, I glanced through the note-pad he'd been using to scrawl in. Most of the scrawls I could read seemed to have some connection with what he'd been telling me about, which I figured must have meant he was thinking about those things deep down. There was my own name, and the names of the targets. I remember one of them was the Kotlass I.C.B.M. base. Then I noticed on one page he'd written down the phrase *Peace on earth*. I looked back through the pages and I found it was written again and again. Not only that, but on one page he'd underlined the initial letters of each word, and written them down below in all their possible six combinations. Right then, something told me that was it. One of them was the code group."

"Hold it," the President said. Franklin had come back into the room. The SAC commander was smiling.

"It worked," Franklin said. "OEP was the correct group. The acknowledgments are coming in now."

The President looked at Zorubin. He could not resist saying, "A pity you won't be able to take up those invitations after all."

The Secretary of State laughed out loud. No-one had ever seen him do that before. The Russian Ambassador beamed. "Perhaps another time," he said mischievously.

"I hope not." The President suddenly realised he was still holding the phone. He covered the mouthpiece with his hand. "Does anyone know this Major Howard?"

"I do," Franklin said. "A good boy. Got brains as well as the ability to fly. There's plenty of room for people like him in the Air Force's T.O."

"He showed a lot of courage insisting on speaking to me personally," the President said slowly. "He worked things out on his own, and he came up with the right answer. I feel we owe him our thanks."

"He must be promoted," Zorubin said emphatically. "He must be made a full colonel at least."

General Steele smiled. "Well no, Your Excellency," he said. "We don't work things quite that way. But when General Franklin reviews the next promotion list for his command, I've no doubt he'll take into consideration what Howard's done today."

"Most certainly," Franklin said.

The President uncovered the mouthpiece of the phone. "Major Howard?"

"Yes, sir?"

"You'll be glad to know your assumption was correct. The group was OEP."

"OEP," Howard muttered. "I suppose that would stand for 'on earth peace', sir?"

"'On earth peace, goodwill to all men,'" the President said quietly. "Yes, it's a variant. Now then, Howard. Before I finish I wish to congratulate you. You've acted in a manner fully in accordance with the highest traditions of your service. The Joint Chiefs, and His Excellency the Russian Ambassador, wish to join their congratulations to mine. I feel sure you'll go a long way in the Air Force."

At Sonora, Howard slowly replaced the phone on its stand. The President's words could only mean he'd be almost certain of a promotion on the next list. So maybe Quinten had known something when he'd scrawled that rank on the note-pad. It was two or three minutes before he remembered he'd forgotten to thank the President, or even acknowledge the message.

The President heard the click at the other end of the line, and replaced his phone with a smile. He walked back round the table to his own seat. Zorubin offered him a cigarette, and he accepted it gravely. He limited his smoking as much as possible, but he felt this was an occasion he could afford to relax his strict regimen.

A constant stream of Air Force aides was coming into the room bearing acknowledgment messages as they were received. General Franklin was ticking off the acknowledgments against the list of bomber numbers.

"How many so far, Franklin?" the President asked.

"Fifteen, sir."

"You consider they will all have received the orders?"

"I don't see why not. Yes, I think they will."

The President glanced at the clock. Two minutes to twelve.

He decided to wait one more minute before he informed the Marshal of their success.

"Let me know as soon as twenty have acknowledged," he instructed Franklin.

"It's seventeen now, sir." Franklin accepted another piece of paper from an aide and marked off two more numbers. "Nineteen now." Another aide came in. Two more ticks were entered on the list. "That makes it twenty-one, Mr. President."

"All right. Zorubin, I'm going to speak to the Marshal now. I may ask you to confirm we have succeeded in re-calling the wing."

"I will be pleased," Zorubin said. Much of the familiar charm was back in his voice the President noted.

The President saw the hands of the clock indicated one minute before twelve. He signalled for the radio link to be opened. Something told him he was going to enjoy the next few minutes.

" ALABAMA ANGEL "

11.55 G.M.T.
Moscow: 2.55 p.m.
Washington: 6.55 a.m.

THERE WAS a saying about flak in world war two. Probably it originated with the R.A.F., because they were the first to experience really heavy flak, and was taken up by the Eighth Air Force later. 'Seeing flak doesn't matter,' it said. 'When you can *hear it*, it's getting close. And when you can *smell* it, you're in trouble.' *Alabama Angel* had been smelling it for ten minutes now, and *Alabama Angel* was in bad trouble.

The first shell to hit had struck somewhere in back of the fuselage. It didn't seem to have done much harm, except the fore and aft controls had become stiffer. It was an effort for Brown to make the small corrections necessary to keep the airplane at a height of two hundred feet.

The second shell had done the real damage. It had exploded between Stan Andersen, standing in the astrodome, and Federov as he stood next to Brown, killing them both. Andersen's body, which had absorbed most of the explosion, was a red, shredded thing on the floor of the cabin. Federov's body had protected Brown, and now slumped against the side panels of the cockpit, the head hanging loosely forward and swinging grotesquely with the movement of the aircraft.

Garcia and Bill Owens had been shocked by the explosion, but Andersen's body had screened them. Physically, they were untouched. Engelbach, forward and crouched over his radar and bombsight, had not felt or heard anything except a sudden, heavy shudder behind him.

Brown was reaching certain conclusions. He knew now that they would never make it out from the target. The numbness was creeping into his upper arms. Movement of the controls was becoming increasingly difficult. He knew that once he had brought the bomber to the target his strength would fail. The alien piece of metal inside him had destroyed his ability to generate fresh power. All that kept him going now was the knowledge he must not fail. Millions of lives depended on his hitting the target and taking it out. He felt as if he were drawing a little power from each one of the millions who depended on him, to keep his weary body working until he hit the primary. He had been planning on Federov taking over then to fly the bomber out. It had been a slim chance. But now Federov was dead, and so was the navigator. The slim chance had become no chance at all.

There was something else. He knew he could not bomb from twenty thousand. It would have to be low level. It did not matter, he thought, because the chance of escape had gone anyway. But did the others know that? Stan Andersen would have known it, but Stan was dead. It was the first time he'd flown without Stan for three years. It didn't make sense somehow that Andersen was there and yet not there, but then war never made sense.

For a few miles ahead the sky was clear, but in the distance clawing up to six thousand feet or more, were more white lines and red explosions. Brown glanced at his watch. A minute before twelve hundred. Almost time to climb to bombing height. Except he hadn't the strength to climb, and he thought it very likely the plane hadn't either. The decision was already made. Now he had to give it to the others.

He said, "Fellows, we have to alter the attack plan. We can't make it to twenty thousand. I'll have to attack from low level. I want you to understand what it means." His voice was very weak against the background crackle of the intercom.

Bill Owens tightened his lips. He knew exactly what Brown meant. As soon as the bomb dropped they had forty seconds to get clear. Forty seconds came out at about six miles. It wasn't far enough, not nearly, to be sure of escaping the blast and heat of the bomb. Dropping from twenty thousand, the plane could turn away immediately while the bomb was still falling towards its target, and be ten or twelve miles away when the explosion took place. At ground level that wasn't possible. He said, "Owens here. I'm in the picture, Clint." His voice was firm and definite, the voice of a man who has accepted what is to come and satisfied it cannot be any other way.

Englebach also realised immediately what the situation was. He gave it little attention. His job was to put the bomb precisely on the target. He would do it. What happened afterwards would happen. Maybe he'd get scared, once he'd let the bomb go. But not right now. Right now he was too busy looking ahead and pinpointing his approach, and computing the distance from the aiming point he'd have to start the mechanisms working. He said, "I understand, Clint." It was the first time he had used Brown's given name in the air. But somehow it seemed like the time to do it.

"O.K., Bill, Harry." Brown paused for a few moments. "How about it, José?"

Garcia flushed. He wasn't used to captains calling him that. But he liked it, he liked it fine. He said, "Too deep for me, Captain."

Brown smiled. Aside from the bomb, Garcia's knowledge was mainly of the kind most useful in bar-rooms and dance halls. He said, "Cut out the Captain malarkey, José. You know my name, now use it."

"Yes, sir," Garcia said. "Clint."

Brown smiled again. Fleetingly. How did it go? All men are equal in the eyes of God? Something like that, A few minutes wasn't going to make any difference. They weren't officers and noncoms now. Just men with a job to do. "Well, this is it, José," he went on. "If we drop from ground level, we just don't have the speed to get far enough away from the burst so the blast doesn't hit us. See what that means?"

Garcia swallowed. He thought of all the bars he'd never entered, the drinks he'd never tried, the girls he'd never made. He looked down at the lifeless shape of Minter, who'd always lent him money when he was broke, and covered up for him when he was adrift. The bars, the drinks, the girls, were kid stuff. This was a man's job, and he was a man doing it. He said, "I get it. Well, if that's the way it has to be, that's the way it is." He paused. Shyness was a new and strange sensation to Garcia, but he was experiencing it now. "Clint," he ended hurriedly.

"Flak's getting pretty close, Clint," Engelbach said.

"O.K. Harry. Bill, you think you can get off the attack groups?"

"I think so. I looked them up here in Meadows' code sheet. Just the aircraft number with AGRB repeated twice to follow it. I can manage that."

Brown sat quietly for a moment. Was there anything he had forgotten? He thought not. Better check on the bomb with Garcia though. "Number one set for maximum delay ground burst, Jose?"

"Maximum delay ground burst, Clint."

"Fine." Brown checked his watch. Three minutes after twelve. The flak rushed nearer. Fifty miles from target. This had to be the last belt of flak. Five minutes more and he could relax, let his pain racked body sink into oblivion. But that was in five minutes more. Now was the flak.

He mustn't forget the attack message to base. Even now, anything could happen. He said, "Bill, I want that message to go out at exactly eight minutes after twelve. If we're still flying then, we'll be through the last flak and almost at the target. Get it off even if we haven't bombed yet. Once the bomb goes down there may not be time.

"Sure," Owens said quietly. "Check time?"

"Twelve zero three and a half."

"Twelve zero three and a half," Owens repeated.

Brown watched two intersecting lines of white tracer forming a bright X directly in his track. The point of intersection of the lines was a good four to five hundred feet above the height he was flying *Alabama Angel*. He took the bomber easily through the lower triangle of the X. From ahead and to starboard another line of tracer came towards him, the shells seeming to move very slowly at first, then suddenly arcing and hissing past the tail of the bomber at dazzling speed.

Quite safe, he thought, they aren't deflecting right. Even radar and electronics didn't solve the aiming problem with their target this far down. It was just as well. He knew he could not have moved his arms sufficiently to take hard evasive action.

"We're on track," Engelbach called. "Fixed the position on that little river back there. Four minutes to run."

"Roger." Brown watched the flak again. He thought they were almost through it now. In front of him a cluster of rockets hissed into the air, to burst and shower burning phosphorus down from two thousand feet. He gauged the distance quickly. They wouldn't affect him. Too far out to port. The airplane topped a small rise, and the ground fell away sharply.

Brown didn't see it in time, and when he did see the danger he moved very slowly and painfully to correct it. For twenty seconds *Alabama Angel* was six hundred feet above ground level. The radar from three light guns locked on to the bomber, the predictors swinging the long barrels ahead of the bomber's nose. Three lines of shells floated lazily towards them.

Brown swore, pushed with all the puny strength he had left at the controls. For an age the bomber remained straight and level, then slowly, as the first shells whipped past her nose, slid down again to the protective nearness of the earth.

Most of the shells passed over the top of the descending bomber. Three did not. One exploded harmlessly in the rear fuselage. One hit a fuel pipe in the starboard wing, and started a fire. The third slammed into the underbelly of the plane, tearing away half of one of the bomb doors.

Alabama Angel rocked under the impacts. But she still flew. And suddenly they were through. Behind them the sky was an inferno of explosives. Ahead, the air was peaceful and empty, and the way to Kotlass was wide open.

Brown glanced at the starboard wing. Burning fuel was sending lashing flames back from the trailing edge of the wing. It didn't matter. They could spare the fuel, and the flames weren't heating anything but air. They were a sitting duck for flak now, with the bright flames a clear give-away of their position. But there wasn't any flak. Brown allowed himself a faint smile of triumph. They'd made it. In just over three minutes Kotlass would cease to exist. So would the bomber, but that didn't matter.

He said quietly, "All right, she's made it. We've got about three minutes left."

Engelbach cleared his throat. He found to his surprise he was not in the least afraid. He said, "Clint, there won't be much time later. Maybe you'd like to say . . ."

The numbness was in Brown's lower arms now. The hand on the controls was insensitive, dead feeling. But he knew it would last out until they were past the target. He said quietly, "Sure, Harry. José, maybe you'd like to stay on your own?"

Garcia remembered back to the tin building in the slums of the Californian town where he had grown up. He remembered the comfort that came when he needed it. He hadn't needed it for years now, or maybe he had and just didn't know it. Now he did. But with Clint Brown, and Harry Engelbach, and Bill Owens. They'd come a long way together in the last two hours. They'd stick together now. He said, "It doesn't seem to matter now, Clint. There's some things right, some wrong, hell I don't know the difference. Say it for me too."

Some things right, some things wrong. Yes, Brown thought, that was it. It was wrong to kill. It was not wrong to defend what you knew was right and good. To attack without cause, to kill without provocation, was wrong. To hit back like they were doing had to be right. He felt a great peace coming on him. What they were doing was surely right, and they could answer for it without shame.

The bomber raced on across the few remaining miles, the long, fierce jet of flame from the starboard wing proclaiming her presence for all to see. Brown began to say a few, very simple words.

THE PENTAGON

12.00 G.M.T.
Moscow: 3 p.m.
Washington: 7 a.m.

"THAT DOES IT," General Franklin said. He had marked the last of the acknowledgements on the list. Only three bombers now remained unaccounted for. They were the two definitely reported as destroyed, and the third hit over the Barents Sea. Obviously that one had been destroyed too. Probably it had crashed into the sea somewhere, and no trace of it would ever be found.

The President was in the middle of a conversation with the Marshal. Franklin wrote a message on a sheet of paper to the effect that twenty-nine bombers had acknowledged, and three had been destroyed. The whole wing was accounted for. He placed the paper in front of the President who nodded and scanned it quickly. Franklin went out of the room to ensure fuelling rendezvous areas had been fixed for the homecoming wing. He had decided to bring them on back to the States. Another wing could rotate overseas in their place.

"Naturally, we will pay compensation for any damage we have caused," the President said. "We will pay for physical damage to Russian property, and we will pay any reasonable compensation for the dependents of those who have lost their lives. Finally, we will take steps to see this can never happen again."

The reply was definite. "It must not happen again. The offer of compensation is accepted."

"If it is within our power to control it, then it will not happen again," the President said firmly. "But I must remind the Marshal we have shown good faith throughout this unfortunate occurrence. Tragedy has only just been averted. We must now make sure it does not occur again, not just by exercising a tighter control on our weapons and commanders, but by removing the root cause from which these incidents may arise. Between us we must reduce international tension. There is no other way. And I repeat, we on our side have already shown good faith."

The reply came almost immediately. "Words are cheap. To pay compensation is easy."

"We are ready to prove our intentions with deeds," the President said quietly. "In fact, I consider we have already done so in the last two hours."

Again the reply was almost immediate. "I wish to ask the President a question. Suppose one of our cities had been destroyed. Would his good faith, his readiness to prove peacable intentions by deeds, have then been so firm he would have allowed one of my bombers free access to a city of his, in fair reprisal for the one an American bomber had destroyed?"

The President pondered. He looked quickly at Zorubin, but the Russian would not meet his glance. "If I considered the peace of the world depended on making that sacrifice, yes I would have allowed it."

"Again I would remind the President that words are cheap."

"My words are never cheap," the President said angrily.

There was silence for all of thirty seconds. Then the Marshal's voice came from the speakers again. The President saw Zorubin blanch as he listened to the harsh but quietly spoken sounds.

Speaking woodenly, and looking straight in front of him, Zorubin said, "The President has stated his words are never cheap. He will now have a chance to show that. Contrary to his assurances, his bombers have not all turned back. One of them is still flying south over Russian territory. We assume its target is the peaceful city of Kotlass. If it hits that city, then I shall ask the President to show that his words are truthful. I shall demand an American city in reprisal."

The President was very pale. "Does he mean it?" he asked Zorubin.

The Russian ambassador said slowly, "Mr. President, I fear so. You must appreciate the Russian system of government. So long as the people see that the Marshal is all-powerful, then he is in no danger. But if a Russian city should be destroyed, and he was not able to say: "There you are. They destroyed one of our cities, and because I am a man of peace I destroyed one of theirs rather than destroying their whole country. Just to teach them a lesson," then he would be in danger of being deposed. You must remember, we are a semi-Asiatic country. Face does not matter to us so much as it does to the Chinese. But it still matters more than it does to you. I am sure he means it."

"The bomber's target isn't the city of Kotlass," General Steele interposed. "It's the I.C.B.M. base outside."

"How far outside?"

"Six miles, Mr. President."

"And the city will be destroyed?"

"If the bomb is within a couple of miles of the aiming point, yes it will be destroyed."

The President drummed his fingers on the table. He saw General Franklin come back into the room and he saw that Franklin had something important to say. "Yes Franklin?"

"Mr. President, the Distant Early Warning stations are reporting Russian bombers. Not many of them, about a dozen. They're holding their position four hundred miles off."

The President frowned. "Zorubin," he said, "If I refuse, what would happen?"

Zorubin shrugged. "It depends. Your bombers are on their way home. He may be tempted to launch an attack, to destroy one or two of your cities regardless of your permission. It would probably be a minor attack, no more than a dozen or so bombers. No doubt those General Franklin has mentioned would be employed."

The President made his decision. "I'll give him a city," he said. "But it shall be a city of my choosing. Further than that I will not go. Franklin, with the state of the prevailing wind, and roughly equating the size of a city to Kotlass, what's the answer?"

Franklin said, "The wind's due west, and likely to stay that way for some time. Mr. President, I'd say Atlantic City. There aren't any visitors this time of year. There are good highways in and out. The population could be evacuated quickly, and any fall-out would be taken away out to sea. If we *have* to give them a city, then that's the best, but I . . ."

"It's my decision, Franklin."

"Yes, sir."

"Keppler?"

"Mr. President."

"I want Atlantic City evacuated right away. I declare martial law in the city, and for an area fifteen miles radius around it. You will take personal charge of the evacuation, and you will act in my name without reference to me. I trust your judgement sufficiently to say here and now I will back any action you take without question."

"Very good, Mr. President." Keppler rose to his feet, a tall, bulky, competent looking man. "One point, sir. Am I to evacuate everyone within the radius of the area you've proclaimed martial law?"

The President looked at the SAC commander. "You're the expert, Franklin. What do you think?"

"It should be enough," Franklin said slowly. "Without looking at the terrain, I couldn't say positively." He paused. "Maybe I should go along with General Keppler. If that is, the general, if he . . ." Franklin came to an embarrassed halt.

"Be glad to have you along," Keppler said warmly. "Don't know anything about these contraptions. Don't want to, either."

"All right then," the President said. "Both of you go. I take it your deputy at Omaha will handle SAC affairs, General Franklin?"

"He's handling them right now, sir."

"All right. Get moving." The President watched Keppler and Franklin leave. He had noted earlier on how Keppler had reacted when Franklin had aligned himself with him during the altercation with Zorubin. If he could do anything to promote good feeling between Army and Air Force generals he felt he should, if only to cut down the number of squabbles he had to umpire in the future.

Now it was time to let the Marshal know his decision. The big wall clock was showing six minutes after twelve. "This is the President," he said quietly. "I wish to inform the Marshal I understand his position if a city of his is destroyed. I consider the peace of the world to be more important than a city on each side. Therefore I am prepared to give one of his bombers free access to an American City of comparable size. I have selected for this purpose Atlantic City. In the event of a Russian city being taken out, one Russian bomber will be permitted to destroy Atlantic City. But I must point out to the Marshal, in that case there would be no question of compensation for the Russian city destroyed. That would be paid for by the death of an American City. It is for him to choose."

The reply took only a few seconds to come. "The President's offer is unacceptable. The American bomber has chosen its target. We wish to choose ours."

"No." The President's tone was unequivocal. "I will not accept that. My offer is final and I will not argue about it. I am ready to go so far to preserve peace. I will not be pushed further."

The men round the table sat very quietly as they waited for the reply. It seemed an age in coming, but in reality it was only a minute or so. "The President's offer is accepted. Can the details be left to the staffs?"

"They can," the President replied shortly. "But it must be understood my permission is conditional on Kotlass being destroyed."

"That is understood."

"Then for the moment there is nothing more to be said." The President relaxed in his chair. The wallclock was showing seven minutes after twelve. One way or another, they would soon know now.

'' ALABAMA ANGEL ''

12.05 G.M.T.
Moscow: 3.05 p.m.
Washington: 7.05 a.m.

AHEAD OF HIM, Clint Brown could see the lights of Kotlass. It was quite dark now at this latitude, but it didn't really matter. The lights were guiding him in. Suddenly as he watched them they went out. All at once, as though someone had operated a master switch and cut the electricity supply off clean at source. Within seconds he found he could still see the town, a vaguely dark mass against the white of the snow covered plains. He continued to fly straight on, confident that the course he was holding would take him over the town and on to the I.C.B.M. base six miles beyond it.

"Time to open bomb doors," Engelbach said calmly.

"Right. Now." Brown thumbed the bomb door release button, while Engelbach manipulated the opening lever. Both controls had to be operated together, otherwise the bomb doors would not open.

"There's something wrong with the circuit lights," Engelbach said urgently. "They haven't gone to green. Hell, they've gone out altogether."

Brown forced his tired mind to concentrate on what Engelbach had said. Something about circuit lights. What did lights matter anyway? He'd felt the slight shudder as the doors came open, and the speed of the plane had dropped off a point or so as it always did. "So the circuits are out. Forget it, Harry."

Brown watched the dark mass of Kotlass coming ever closer. Now it was time for the last routine drill, the one he'd hoped he'd never have to go through. "O.K. José, let's make her live."

"Opening firing circuit," Garcia said.

"Roger." Brown unlocked his master switch, and pulled down on the red lever. Immediately a harsh red light glowed at the top of the instrument panel. Brown mustered just enough strength to force one of his deadening hands to fumble with the rheostat and dim the glaring brightness of the light.

It was done. The bomb was live. Only one safety device now remained, in the shape of two slim steel pegs which connected the fuselage of the plane with two vital parts deep inside the bomb. When the bomb fell away, the two steel pegs would be left, and as they slid out of the falling bomb they would open the trigger primer circuits. Once that happened, the bomb would explode as soon as the pre-set height had been reached. For this particular bomb that meant forty seconds after being dropped, which was the maximum delay after the pre-set height, because it would be dropped near enough the pre-set height anyway.

Kotlass came closer, rushing towards them through the Arctic night. Dimly, Brown felt a vague pity for the people there who had only a few seconds more of life left to them. But he could not spare much thought for them. His hands were numb now, and his vision was becoming misty. It was an effort to say, "Bill, get the message out."

Owens applied himself to the unfamiliar task of radio transmission. He manipulated the key slowly and carefully. He felt confident he had not made a mistake. "I got it out, Clint," he said, just as the town of Kotlass rushed past beneath them.

Engelbach looked ahead. His target radar was indicating some obstruction five miles ahead and slightly off to starboard. He strained to pierce the darkness and identify it.

He checked his bomb release mechanisms, and found them working perfectly. Suddenly he saw the obstruction his radar indicated. It was a launching tower, reaching high in the air, its top lost in the darkness. Engelbach felt a surging elation. They'd made it. In five seconds he would bomb, and he'd guarantee he'd lay it within a half mile of the aiming point.

His hand went to the release switch. "Release switch, Clint," he said.

"Release switch." Brown summoned all his dying resolution. He had to lift his hand, and move it forward six inches. It was impossible. He lifted it. He could not move it forward, he simply could not. Inch by painful inch he moved it forward. Now, he was touching the switch. Pull it down. The cabin was filling with blackness, thick blackness in which he was swimming. He could not see the switch. He had forgotten what it was for. He knew only his life would have been futile unless he operated it. He pulled firmly down and slumped back in his seat, the hand which had pulled the switch hanging limply by his side.

A green light glowed in Engelbach's bomb release panel. He saw another launching tower away to port, and he knew he was almost at the aiming point. He pressed the bomb release button and said quietly, "Bomb gone."

THE PENTAGON

12.07 G.M.T.
Moscow: 3.07 p.m.
Washington: 7.07 a.m.

IN Moscow it was dark now, in Washington just light. The Pentagon and the Kremlin were separated by eight hours of time, and forty years of mutual mistrust. The link between them was as fragile and tenuous as the radio beam which carried their messages to and fro.

In the Pentagon, the President consulted with General Steele about the fate of Atlantic City. They decided there would be plenty of time to evacuate the population. The Russian bombers reported by the DEW line could not possibly get there in under three to four hours. Civil Defence had already started on the evacuation, while Keppler and Franklin were still on their way by helicopter to Marshal Field, where a jet bomber was waiting for them.

The President could not see he had had any alternative but to sacrifice a city. Zorubin should know just how the Marshal would act, and Zorubin had been positive the Marshal would feel he must have an American city if Kotlass was destroyed. The clock moved on to eight minutes after twelve. There was just the one faint hope, the President felt, that even now the Russians might manage to destroy the last bomber. No matter how faint, it was still a chance. He grasped at it eagerly.

"The Russians report it's still heading in," Steele said quietly, as though he were reading the President's mind. He saw a worried frown cross the President's face, and went on quickly, "Of course, there's a time lag in communications. Four or five minutes at least before the reports from their stations are filtered through the Kremlin and passed on to us."

"Would the same time lag apply to communications from our bombers also?"

"Yes it would, but not in so great a degree. We were getting the acknowledgements on paper here within two minutes of transmission."

The President looked at the clock. Nine minutes after, now. "And you're sure the bomber would send an attack message when it bombed?"

Steele shrugged. "It's difficult to say. The way I see it, this bomber has been hit. Maybe the radio's smashed. That would account for it not picking up the recall message. I'm afraid we can't rely on it transmitting, sir."

"No, of course. Then the first news is likely to come from them?"

"Probably. Incidentally, those Russian bombers are still holding their position." Steele looked carefully at the President. "The long range fighters from Thule could reach them quite easily," he said with an elaborate casualness. "It's one thing to mount a reprisal with forces already available, quite another if you have to get more planes off the ground and send them over the ice cap."

"I don't think we can do that," the President said slowly.

Steele thought he detected a slight hesitancy in the President's voice. "I only meant it would give time for second thoughts," he said. "Time for tempers to cool off."

"It might also give time for the position to revert to what it was an hour ago," the President said grimly. "No, Steele, it can't be done. I've given my word. Now I have to stand by it, if ever we're to salvage something of international relations from this mess." He turned away to talk to Zorubin.

Well, Steele thought, that was it. He had no doubt himself the bomber would reach its target. It was probably a little behind schedule, but that was natural if it had been hit. Ten after twelve now. Add four minutes for the time lag, plus maybe another minute for the inevitable reporting delay the shock of the explosion would cause. And bomb time for that aircraft was one minute after to nine minutes after. The next six minutes should bring something in.

He was interrupted by an aide. "General, the Russians report the bomber as through the last defence sector. They say it's on fire and down to a hundred meters, but it's heading straight for Kotlass."

"Thank you," Steele said. He wondered if he should pass the news on to the President. He decided not. The news of the explosion would come soon enough now. He closed his eyes for a moment and imagined what the crew of the bomber must be feeling. They were down to three hundred feet. Why? Probably because they'd been hit bad and couldn't fly any higher. But in that case they'd be caught by the blast of the explosion. Yet they were going in at the target regardless of the fact when they killed it they would inevitably kill themselves too. At that moment Steele felt an even greater than normal pride in his Air Force. And a bitter sorrow that kids had to die that way.

Zorubin was talking to the President. In the last ninety minutes he felt he had come very close to this stooped, scholarly man. He had been immensely impressed with the firm grasp the President had on the reins of government. He achieved absolute command without his leadership becoming obtrusive or unpleasant. Yet he was instantly obeyed.

The Russian Ambassador had noted, too, the stubborn determination the President had shown when he refused pointblank to allow the Marshal to choose an American city. The refusal had been couched in moderate language, but it was no less firm for all that. Zorubin made a mental note for future reference that the President could be pushed only so far. Once he reached the limit he had set he dug his heels in. To attempt to push him further might be dangerous. Extremely dangerous. Zorubin had learned a great deal in the past hour. He wondered if the implications of what had happened had yet struck the President. Zorubin, behind a mask of ignorance, concealed a high degree of general knowledge of missiles, and their guidance systems, and the production difficulties associated with them.

He saw an aide approach General Steele, and hand him a message sheet. Steele read it quickly, his face impassive. He walked over to where Zorubin and the President stood together. Just as he reached them the wall clock clicked on to eleven minutes after twelve.

"Mr. President, Your Excellency," Steele said formally, "I have here a message from the one bomber of the eight forty-third we have been unable to contact. It says merely that the bomber has attacked. The time of origin is nine minutes after twelve."

"Thank you," the President said quietly. His expression was sad. The last chance had gone.

"ALABAMA ANGEL"

12.10 G.M.T.
Moscow: 3.10 p.m.
Washington: 7.10 a.m.

ENGELBACH slowly relaxed his pressure on the bomb release button. Already the count-down clock was showing only thirty-five seconds before detonation. Engelbach recalled a book he had read somewhere about the way executions were carried out in various countries. The British, he remembered, still executed their murderers by hanging. They prided themselves on the efficiency of their system. Inside thirty seconds after the executioner entered the cell, he had read, the convicted man was dead. Apparently it never bothered the man who was to be hung. The time interval was too short. All right, Engelbach thought, it wouldn't bother him either. He watched the racing second hand sweep past thirty. Now he would discover for himself just how a man did feel. So far he was fine.

Bill Owens was looking up at the stars. There were so many of them, he thought, and they were so remote. As soon as he had sent out the attack message he had gone to stand in the astrodome, where Stan Andersen had been standing when the shell had killed him. Owens thought about Andersen. A hell of a nice guy, Stan. Always a little reserved, but dependable in a tight corner. A nice guy. Owens picked out the planet Mars. Maybe he was a little colour blind, but he'd never been able to detect the red tint other people said it had. He rememberd when he was a boy he'd gone with his grandpa to the top of a hill near where they lived, and grandpa had brought his telescope along. It was a beautiful telescope, all shining brass and polished lenses. They'd looked for the men who were supposed to live on Mars, and he'd been disappointed when they couldn't see any. He smiled in remembrance of his childish disappointment. In a way he was lucky. Pretty soon he'd know all about Mars, and the other stars and planets too. He's see Stan Andersen again. There couldn't be more than twenty seconds left now. Maybe he'd see Grandpa, as well. He turned in the astrodome, trying to locate the Square of Pegasus. He was content.

Garcia was thinking about a girl in Dallas. He was not thinking of her in any tender way, but with a sense of the infinite fitness of things. She thought she was going to blame him, just because she could produce a bell-hop ready to swear he'd seen them together in a room at the Laredo Hotel where he'd been stupid enough—or maybe drunk enough—to register his correct name and address. As if he didn't know she was on the make for any serviceman who came into town with a full billfold. Well, she'd have a long way to travel to get any money from him now. He laughed with pure delight. He felt very glad he was going to preserve his record right to the end.

Engelbach, Owens, and Garcia were all content. They were not frightened, because they already counted themselves dead, and had done so ever since Clint Brown said he would have to bomb at low level. They were content, and they had made their peace. The seconds could tick away as fast as they liked.

Clint Brown was actually dead. His last living act had been to depress the release switch which had enabled Engelbach to drop the bomb. When Engelbach pressed the button Brown was already dead, the ultimate reserves of vitality drained from him with the constant loss of blood from his shattered back.

He had trimmed the aircraft for level flight, and so *Alabama Angel* continued to fly. Very gradually, with a shifting of weight when Engelbach had pressed the button, she had eased round to a south-easterly heading. And she was flying slightly higher now as the ground fell away beneath her. The green light on the radio altimeter glowed, and then abruptly winked out. Seconds later the red light came on. The declination of the ground was past, and now it was sloping gently up to meet the bomber again.

Thirty-five seconds after bomb release point, and nearly six miles from the aiming point, *Alabama Angel* brushed against the sloping ground. She began to break up, but the impact bounced her up to six hundred feet as she did. Pieces fell away from the stricken airplane, among them the nose section with Engelbach still in it. The main fuselage split open, and something heavy, and cylindrical, fell from the bomb bay, where it had been retained by the wreckage of one of the bomb doors.

The steel pegs were left in the bomber and the bomb, its stabilising fins torn off as it dropped from the plane, turned over twice in the air before hitting the ground and bouncing. Without the stabilising fins to steady it in its descent it fell end over end, and when it struck the ground the outer steel casing burst open. The bomb bounced to a hundred feet and fell back. As it hit for the second time the outer casing broke away, and the core of the bomb tore into a ragged line of conifers before it came to rest.

Alabama Angel hit the same line of conifers, the wings tearing off as the fuselage disintegrated under the impact. Owens and Garcia died in the instant explosion of the fuel tanks, Engelbach a second or two later as the nose section thumped into the ground. Flames leapt three hundred feet in the air as all that was left of *Alabama Angel* burned.

Thirty seconds after the original impact, the high explosive cartridges hurled together the two plutonium masses. Instantly an atomic explosion occurred, and the tritium core was ignited. But the deuterium filling, which constituted the main charge, had gone with the disintegration of the steel casing. An explosion certainly occurred, and one which was fifteen or twenty times more potent than the bomb which had wrecked Hiroshima. But the main charge was not detonated, because it was no longer there to be detonated.

The explosion was seen by another B-52 of the 843rd Wing, which was heading north-west after receiving a recall while on its way to hit a bomber base at Glasov on the Chepza river. The navigator fixed the position of the explosion exactly, and the radioman got off a message giving the details.

The wreckage of *Alabama Angel* was completely disintegrated by the explosion, and an area of one mile radius from the centre was turned into a white hot, seething inferno. Thirty seconds after the explosion, the familiar mushroom cloud had burst up to fifty thousand feet. At its base, the crew of *Alabama Angel* slept their last sleep. They had failed, yet in their failure they had achieved victory. They could sleep content.

THE PENTAGON

12.15 G.M.T.
Moscow: 3.15 p.m.
Washington: 7.15 a.m.

"I AM INFORMED the bomber which we reported as still heading in towards Kotlass has made its attack. An explosion has occurred." Zorubin translated smoothly and fluently, transmuting the harsh sounds from the speaker into precise, diplomatic English. "Does the President stand by his agreement that one of his cities shall now be destroyed?"

The President closed his eyes for a moment. Well, this was it. He had given his word, and now he must stand by it. "Yes," he said curtly, "I do."

"Very well then, let us set a time. I propose fifteen minutes from now. That will be at 7.30 your time."

The President nodded absently. He became, aware of Steele waving a hand in sudden agitation. Fifteen minutes from now. *Fifteen minutes!* There was some mistake. The evacuation of Atlantic City would not be anywhere near complete. "You have made a mistake in time," he said. "The staffs have agreed that your bomber cannot be in position much before ten o'clock our time."

Thirty seconds went by while the President's words were translated in the Kremlin. Then the speakers began to crackle again. Zorubin translated quickly and continuously as the message came over. "I have overruled the staff proposals. Atlantic City will not be destroyed by bomber. It will be destroyed by a missile from a submarine which is lying four hundred miles off your coast. Orders have been given to the submarine commander he is to fire his missile at 7.25 your time. It will take about five minutes to reach its target." Zorubin's voice was flat. He appreciated exactly the significance of the message. In something under fifteen minutes at least fifty thousand people would die in Atlantic City.

The President swayed. For a moment he felt the onset of actual physical nausea. He fought it down and clutched at the table in front of him to steady himself. He looked across at Admiral Maclellan. "Well?" he asked. His face was white.

Maclellan said quietly, "It could be, sir. They usually have one or two subs lying off four hundred or so miles out. The missiles they carry have that much range."

"And accuracy?"

Maclellan frowned. "At four hundred miles not good. Between five and ten miles."

"I see." The President signalled for the radio link to be opened. "The Marshal's proposal is unacceptable," he said quietly. "Atlantic City has not yet been evacuated."

The reply came quickly. "Neither had the city of Kotlass."

"It is not solely for that reason the proposal is unacceptable," the President said. "I am informed the missiles carried by Russian submarines are not sufficiently accurate to guarantee a hit on target at four hundred miles. The agreement was that Atlantic City should be hit and nowhere else. I must ask the Marshal to suggest an alternative method."

Again the reply was quick. "They are sufficiently accurate." There was a short pause, and when the next sentence was spoken there was no mistaking the bitterness and determination of the voice. "I will not consider any alternative. The missile will be fired seven minutes from now."

"Zorubin," the President said quietly, "I have been trapped. You realise what it will mean if the missile is fired?"

"I do." Zorubin's voice was low. "And I am sorry. But it seems his mind is made up. I can tell."

The President thought for a moment of the SAC wings which were still airborne, of the bombers of the 843rd which, many of them, were still over Russian territory. It would be so easy for him to threaten action. And so futile. The position had not changed in the last hour or so. The ultimate threat still lay beneath the Urals, ready at any moment to poison the world. He thought too, after all a Russian city had been destroyed. If it had been his own decision he would not have insisted on a meaningless reprisal. But it was not his decision, and perhaps to the man in the Kremlin it was not meaningless. He waved a hand for the radio link to be opened.

"Wait!" General Steele's voice was loud and sharp. "Mr. President, wait a minute."

The President looked at him. Steele held a message form in his hand. "Well, Steele?" he asked.

"Kotlass was not destroyed, Mr. President. Neither the city nor the I.C.B.M. base. This message is from a SAC crew who actually saw the explosion, as they were heading out after recall. They state definitely the explosion occurred fifteen miles south-east of the city of Kotlass, in an entirely uninhabited area. They further state the explosion was a small one, in the kiloton rather than megaton range."

"I don't understand," the President said slowly. "They were carrying the normal weapons, I take it?"

"They were, sir. This is just guesswork, but I'd say what happened was this. We know the particular bomber was hit, and we know from what the Russians told us it was flying at very low level. It could well have suffered damage to some of the bomb release mechanisms and carried the bomb on past the target. Then, when the bomb dropped, it may not have had time to stabilise itself in flight, and perhaps hit the ground in such a way the primer exploded but not the main charge. That would cause an explosion in the kiloton range. Say between one and two hundred kilotons."

"And that is technically possible?"

"It is," Steele said. "What the report means, Mr. President, is that no city has been destroyed, and no military base. The actual explosion probably caused no casualties at all. There'll be a fall out hazard, of course, but nothing compared with an H-bomb explosion. If they get to work quickly they should be able to evacuate in plenty of time to avoid radiation casualties."

"Has the report been confirmed?"

"It has sir."

"Very well." The President's voice was full of new hope. He glanced at the clock. Six minutes to go before the missile was fired. There was time. He saw the green light wink on to indicate the opening of the link for him.

"I have just received a report," he said, "which enables me to request the Marshal to cancel his orders to the submarine. I suggest this be done as a matter of urgency. The report gives the news that the town of Kotlass was quite untouched by the explosion. Further, the explosion itself was a comparatively small one, of the kind usually associated with atomic rather than hydrogen weapons. I am sure the Marshal will join me in expressing satisfaction that Kotlass has been spared, and Atlantic City can be spared too."

"I know nothing of that. The missile will be fired," the reply said flatly.

"But Kotlass was unharmed," the President said quickly.

"I know nothing of that. Your bomber dropped its bomb. My submarine will fire its missile."

The President turned away abruptly. He was fighting to control himself, to hold back the bitter words which were shaping themselves on his tongue. "It had better not," he said at last. His voice was calm, but it had in it a note of bitterness which had never been there before. "I gave my word that I would give a city for the one destroyed. Your city has not been destroyed. And so I will not accept the destruction of Atlantic City. That is all I have to say."

Zorubin looked carefully at the President. He realised instantly that the President had reached the brink. He could be pushed no further. Zorubin sensed that in the final analysis the President would not now hesitate to take action. Once again, the fate of the world was trembling in the balance. But did the Marshal know that? Or was he merely playing a cynical game of bluff, under the impression the President was bluffing too? Zorubin made up his mind.

He stepped forward. "Excuse me, Mr. President," he said formally. "I wish to speak to the Marshal direct." He flicked his fingers for the opening of the link. The green light winked on. Before anyone in the room could recover from the surprise of his action, Zorubin was speaking in Russian.

He spoke fast but clearly, pausing twice to allow questions to be put from Moscow. For nearly two minutes the conversation continued. Zorubin finished with a long burst of speech followed by a single sentence whose intonation made it clear he was asking a question. He waited impassively for the answer. Finally it came, a sharp monosyllable.

Zorubin turned to the President. His forehead was glistening with perspiration. But he was smiling. "The missile will not be fired, Mr. President. The Marshal states he had no real intention of firing it. He merely wished to make sure you and your staff knew what it was to see a city of yours in immediate danger of destruction."

"I see," the President said thoughtfully. "I must thank you, Your Excellency, for your good offices."

Zorubin formally bowed his appreciation. It had been very close, he thought. Only the trust which his old friend placed in his evaluation of the situation had enabled him to obtain the cancellation of the firing order. The Marshal had been quite sure the President would do no more than protest the action. Zorubin had assured him differently. And fortunately the Marshal had believed him.

"Now," the President said. "We must take steps immediately to see this does not happen again. Steele."

"Sir?"

"Plan R must be abolished. See to that immediately."

Steele shrugged. He would carry out the President's order, but he felt compelled to point out the removal of plan R would leave a gap in the defences. He did so.

The President heard him out. Then he said, "I think not. I venture to think the events of the last two hours have shown that a Russian attack on this country will not now take place. Not in our time, at least."

Zorubin looked at him sharply. He thought that the President had probably assessed the situation correctly. He wondered just how he had arrived at his conclusion.

"The Russians have a lead with the I.C.B.M.," the President said slowly. "We will need six months or so before our Minuteman sites will be ready, so that retaliation would become inevitable and infallible. On that day, I believe, war will not only become impossible but will be recognised by both sides as such."

"That is in six months," Steele said stiffly. "For at least four months of that period they will have their long range missiles ready and we will not. They know that."

"Yes, but they know other things too. Or at least," the President turned and looked at Zorubin, "they will know. For example, they already know they cannot stop the 52.K's with their radar-guided missiles. I would not think they could replace their radar missiles inside a period of six months with missiles which are still experimental."

Zorubin's eyes flickered for just a moment. He was conscious of the President's keenly assessing gaze. He smiled. The President had spotted the obvious flaw in the Russian position.

"Then again," the President continued, "they know the second wing of K's become operational this month, and a third next month. They will also know, as soon as His Excellency's report reaches them, that from now until the time our Minuteman sites are operational, I am ordering a force of at least twenty bombers of the K type to be airborne twenty-four hours of each day, fully armed. They will not head for their X points, but remain in the refuelling areas. They will be under my direct control. They will guarantee the peace, until the Minuteman sites make peace inevitable. And peace, gentlemen, I am determined to create."

Zorubin's voice was quiet as he said, "The President is correct. Once both sides have missiles which will automatically retaliate, war becomes profitless. If it is profitless, it will not be fought." He shrugged. "Ideological differences are not so sharply defined as the line between life and death. We may have to learn how to differ. But better that than having to learn how to die."

"Exactly," the President said. "And now gentlemen, I wish to speak privately with the Russian Ambassador and the Secretary of State. I have promised compensation for any damage caused. I shall probably go to Moscow to discuss details with the Marshal. The Ambassador and I will make arrangements with him immediately. Thank you all for your help."

Zorubin watched the service officers and aides file out of the room. He thought this could well be the beginning of a new era. On both sides, Russian and American, the men who counted had lived through two hours of fear. It had not been theoretical fear, the kind of fear any sane man felt when he contemplated the destruction potential of the two opposing camps. It had been genuine, inescapable fear of the logical end to a course of events which they had seemed powerless to prevent. No-one, on either side, could live through a time like that and ever again seek war.

"You know," the President said, "the general who actually launched the attack did so because he was convinced it was the only way to secure peace on earth."

Zorubin considered the President's words for a moment. "Well," he said, "his attack failed. But I'm not sure it hasn't resulted in securing peace on earth just the same."

"Let's hope so." The President sank into the seat he had used during the action. He was very weary, but he felt that his biggest effort was still to come. Yet he looked forward to it. He felt, like Zorubin, that no-one who had lived through that time could ever again take any action which might lead to war. "Let's make it so," he said determinedly. He signalled for the link to be opened, and began to talk to the Marshal.

The End

Made in the USA
Middletown, DE
06 January 2022